Canon Of The Non-Sacred Writings

Five New Sherlock Holmes Cases

By

Richard K. Tobin

Paperback ISBN 978-1-78705-127-0
ePub ISBN 978-1-78705-128-7
PDF ISBN 978-1-78705-129-4

Published in the UK by MX Publishing
335 Princess Park Manor, Royal Drive,
London, N11 3GX
www.mxpublishing.co.uk

Cover design by Brian Belanger

I started writing in my retirement years as I cared for my ailing mother. Her favorite comment to my siblings was 'Mordecai is taking good care of me'. The pet name was taken from our famous Canadian author Mordecai Richler. I dedicate this book to my mother for her unfailing encouragement and support. May her afterlife be just as wonderful as she believed.

Contents

Once a Mountie Always a Mountie

"Yes, you are right, American women are good looking. I found that out by taking short walks around New York when I had a few minutes of unoccupied time.

I learned more respect for your country by walking your streets.

"And you are staying three nights you say Mr. Rippa?"

The desk clerk Sal, looked at me curiously.

He struck me as part Italian, perhaps some Indian Blood. Regardless, he had a dark complexion. His black hair was plastered to his scalp and swept back in a wave on the right side of his head. I told the desk clerk to just call me Monty. He was the personable sort, asking questions about the nature of my visit and wondering if he could assist me in any way.

I went on. "I practice nursing in Canada after 8 years of police work with the Mounties."

"Mounties, I am not that sure about what I know of the Mounties."

I said, "They are officially known as the Royal Canadian

Mounted Police. They are Canada's official national police coast to coast. I don't count too much anymore in the RCMP world. I gave it up for the less strenuous life of a nurse. I can now relax some of the time."

"A Mountie friend of mine was murdered. I was going to quit my police job and become a nurse but I postponed it in the hope that I could help find the murderer and bring him to justice. Hopefully he would be given a long time in prison. That's worse than dying in my opinion. After my friend's murder, I thought of becoming a nurse more seriously."

The desk clerk whose full name was Sal Della Vella said, "When I come across a good crime story I will at times send it into one of the local newspapers who do not mind amateurs sending in true crime stories."

As I finished checking in Sal said that he was through for the day if I wanted to meet him in the hotels lounge for a drink. Sal seemed interested in my past work with the RCMP and he was most likely wondering the purpose of my visit to New York.

I replied, "Yes, let's continue our conversation Sal. I will just run my suitcase up to my room first, and come down to join you."

Sal said, "I am looking forward to it, and to be truthful I am hoping to hear a crime story or two."

I had to laugh. I was soon sitting across from Sal and we talked easily like old friends. He was attending college in the evenings but he soon switched the conversation back to my short career with the R.C.M.P. I told him my favorite story of that time in my life.

A few months after a friend of mine was murdered, who arrived in Halifax where I was posted but Sir Arthur Conan Doyle. He had to stop over in Halifax, it not only being the capital city of Nova Scotia, but an excellent seaport as well. It was to be a brief stopover until he continued his journey to New York City.

You may know that Sir Arthur created the famous Detective Sherlock Holmes and not his sidekick and valued friend Dr. Watson."

Sal replied, "Yes I have read a couple of them. I read two or three of his mystery stories. They sell on this side of the Atlantic."

I delved into my story. "All the Mounties in Halifax

were instructed to ensure that Sir Arthur had a pleasant and uneventful stay in Halifax. He was going to New York, to iron out difficulties with royalty payments with an important American publisher and to sign a new deal of one kind or another. Also, since he had a bit of time he planned to see Halifax and this part of the world. He was even thinking of visiting Toronto and Montreal, two big Canadian cities.

As I learned our inspector and a couple of our top Sergeants were with Sir Arthur for the duration of his visit. His books sold well in Canada and he was considered a celebrity in our part of the world.

As it turned out, the great writer had heard of the murder of my friend. He was always interested when an officer of the law was murdered. Sir Arthur believed that a strong police force would help a city prosper and grow with the citizens feeling safe and secure in a peaceful environment. Feelings of safety and security free a citizenry, leaving them with energy to build and grow their community.

For my part, I knew where he would be having lunch and since the restaurant was on my beat, I timed my foot patrol for as close as I could to lunchtime.

As luck would have it the lunch party arrived by car just as I was no more than twenty feet away. More than one of Sir Arthur's entourage recognized me, including Sergeant Gibbons."

Surprisingly as we sipped on our drinks Sal turned out to be a good listener. I would try not to disappoint him with my story of how Sir Arthur Conan Doyle helped solve the murder of an RCMP officer in Halifax, Nova Scotia.

Sal encouraged the continuation of the story; "This is getting very interesting."

Sir Arthur Conan Doyle and his literary agent were set to enjoy a pleasant lunch enjoying East Coast Canada pub culture. I booked off work and I didn't want the visitors and dignitaries to wonder why I was having a leisurely lunch so I explained I was just off duty after having to work a little overtime. I decided "what the hell" and joined the group in the pub. I ordered a twelve ounce mug of draft beer. I introduced myself to the dignitaries and they indicated that the group had already discussed my efforts to find my friend and colleague's killer.

Sir Arthur noted, "You came to our attention earlier. The one thing that set you apart from other policemen is your dedication. The Sergeants both discussed that you postponed nursing school entry and that you remained in the RCMP to continue the investigation into the murder of your Mountie friend. I understand that you have an eyewitness account of the murder. Scotland Yard now uses an artist to interview the witnesses and develop a sketch of the killer. Investigating officers use the sketch to see if the killer is recognized by other likely witnesses or to see if someone can put a name to the face. I was impressed by the ingenuity of Scotland Yard and I could see the value to this idea."

Sal interrupted, "This rates another drink. You should take up writing. So far what I am hearing is a thousand dollars story. Tell about that sketch."

I replied, "The sketch plays an important role later in the story."

First I glanced around at the lounge. It was in good shape, clean and well repaired. The walls and ceiling looked freshly painted. The floor was of linoleum and masterfully installed seams free.

Sal looked slim but wiry, his nose was crooked but still a decent looking guy. I took a sip of my beer and started in.

"Getting back to the death of our RCMP officer, the killer up on his motorcycle, American made no doubt, thanks to a certain Nikolaus Otto who invented the internal combustion engine some years ago, he was wearing brown cowboy boots and denim pants and matching jacket. That alone marked him as a radical."

Sal interrupted, "That could have been an Indian motorbike. They are produced in New Jersey."

I replied, "The killer pulled out a rifle from his bike and shot my friend to death."

After a brief pause I mentioned to Sal, "How I wish I knew Kate, my girlfriend at that time. She would have known how to help support me in my grief. I muddled through it, although not without a lot of help."

Sal smiled and nodded.

Then I mentioned, "I am so near to the end of my story I will carry on."

I felt bad when I heard a few years ago that Sherlock's creator had died. He was still fairly young. I did appreciate Sir Arthur's help.

OK Sal, back to the pub, Sir Arthur offered, "Show your drawing sketch as it were to the school authorities it might prod their memories. If you have contacts with the underworld ask them about the sketch. Tell the school authorities and others that he is radically anti social. Society is corrupt to him."

I asked, "What about me contacting radical organizations like the communist party?"

Sir Arthur replied, "You could but would they help or hinder? Perhaps go in under cover. Look for a man who is usually a loner."

"I did keep looking on."

Sal interrupted the story to point out two beautiful women, "Those damn women had you and I divided up ten minutes ago." I looked and the brunette was looking over her right shoulder at me. The blonde was more than interested in Sal.

I said, "Do not remind me that this is my last few days of freedom. I am soon to be married.

Sal replied, "Do nothing, they hate it when they have to do all the work. But about the story, I sense a fortune in the offing."

I followed Sir Arthur's advice and I kept looking in all the usual places. I was regularly stymied in all the places where the locals turned to crime. I persisted and headed into the hobo jungle in the South End near where the railway handles their Cape Breton run. This time though I went in with backup. My partner Jake joined me for this excursion.

While my backup Jake kept an eye peeled for trouble, I looked around. Two women there were wearing white blouses, somewhat soiled skirts often worn by office girls. Three red eyed men were passing around a bottle of cheap wine. I quickly sensed from the reactions I received from this group that I was on the right track. I squeezed the group a bit harder and got the name George Henry.

We continued deeper into Hobo Alley. As I suspected, sitting on the ground was, I presumed George Henry. There was one more piece of evidence to check. The eye witnesses sketch had a three inch long scar just below Henry's right ear. I checked and the scar was visible and just as the eye witnesses had described, narrow at the top and wider at the bottom. What I had to contend with was a violent man. I told him why I was here yet had no trouble putting the cuffs on him.

George Henry was strung out on drugs and probably

delusional. He killed my friend most likely in this exact frame of mind. He was in rough shape, urgently needing a bath and a shave.

At the Royal Canadian Mounted Police station he was questioned and was cooperative but refused to sign a confession. He claimed it might interfere with him getting a fair trial. He did not answer me when I asked him why he killed my friend!!

Sal said, "What an interesting story but how did the trial go?"

I replied, "I was satisfied. He was given life in prison. As a cop killer his time in prison might be too comfortable!"

Sal remarked, "You must feel satisfied!"

I paused and reflected. I remembered Sir Arthur asking me if I wanted to solve the murder. I told him that I wanted to solve the murder of my friend so bad that I could taste it.

But then again, once a Mountie always a Mountie.

A Pregnant Pause In Time

It was turning dark so I decided I had best turn toward home. It was a solitary trip, my friend, and partner, Holmes having come down with influenza.

I had spent a few hours reliving the past by walking about my old neighbourhood where I once practiced medicine. This was prior to throwing in my lot with Holmes, one of the U.K.'s most reputable private detectives.

I was walking towards Avion Row where there was always an unoccupied Hansom or two passing by or on occasion, one of these new motorized cabs. The cabs were starting to become popular but I didn't care, it was just time I was home.

Directly across the street was an old bootmaker's shop. The bootmaker was quite vocal claiming loudly that he was losing business because of these new prefabricated boots that were being sold in shoe stores rather than by the artisan who had made them. This new method didn't come with the artisan's reputation attached to the boot so a buyer had to choose carefully.

As I walked about the old neighbourhood no one seemed to recognize me. I was half hoping someone would come up to me and ask, aren't you Dr. Watson, but no one did. Even the barman earlier on didn't seem to recognize me. He resembled a young waiter who worked in the bar on what few occasions I had to visit a bar.

This night there was a mysterious, quite unusual looking woman standing in front of the bootmaker's building. Oddly enough, she was staring at me.

That piqued my curiosity and I made note of her. She was a tall woman with long, light brown hair. Two things made her unique. Thanks to a lamppost very near where she was standing and my unusually strong eyes I saw where she had a scar on the right side of her face about two inches long and a half an inch wide. The other difference in her appearance was that she had large breasts, not inordinately so, but prominent in a standout way.

She seemed somehow to be familiar to me. Perhaps I had treated her at one time or another but my practice had been closed for what was now eighteen years or thereabouts.

I continued onward to Avion Row, when after several

paces a young blonde woman, this one also with fairly prominent breasts as well; stepped out of a doorway directly into my path. Was it a coincidence, perhaps not? But this woman was also looking directly at me.

As I walked by I said, "Excuse me, Madam."

"Oh, well, you'll have to forgive me sir but I feel somehow that you can help me."

"Perhaps not as much as you think."

The young blonde said, "My first name is Alva and my last name is Puddicome. Far from an illustrious last name. The reason I mention it is my brother Ralph Puddicome has disappeared. Even the police don't know where he is.

He had this girlfriend, Eve, who was trying to get him to join the Salvation Army. He has yet to join and I'm wondering if something foul has happened to him. His girlfriend is religious. She may have caused trouble for him."

I asked, "Have you heard from him at all?"

"No, he used to work further down the street at Bobbing's Laundry. It only pays the minimum despite being hard work. That's another reason why I worry. He is tall but very skinny. He's not quite frail but weak. He could have worked himself to death for all I know or he may be hospitalized."

"I see." I replied, "I don't know much about these matters." Whatever this particular matter might be, but I decided to play along. It might be in my best interest to do so. Of course, I remained suspicious of her motivations and how I was chosen to be of help.

I said, "I do have a friend who has done detective work but he has been afflicted with influenza. However, if you like I will ask around on my own."

If nothing else, this way I could come to the bottom of these hard stares and see if this cleavage festooned on both women is natural or not. They could both be prostitutes. I couldn't help but feel that there was a blood relationship between both women. However, I did make note of the fact that the blonde had black roots. As for the missing brother, I was doubtful if he had gone very far. In the meantime, he was my interest as I looked to fill a few hours. I very rarely ventured on my own, but I saw no harm coming from this matter.

The young woman said now looking away from me, "I

can pay you some money if you look for Ralph, more if you're successful."

"No," I replied. "I'm more of an out of work doctor. Matter of fact I used to practice near here."

The young blonde in a spurt of anger said, "You admit to being a God-awful quack of the worst kind."

Taken aback I said, "No, no, not at all."

She had regained control and said, "I suppose, yes, just my imaginings that probably aren't true."

I could only wonder about the outburst. This woman was too hard to meltdown from her rigidity.

I soon returned to my comfortable home and the housekeeper had left water on for tea. There was also a sandwich wrapped in wax paper in case I came home hungry.

I sat in my chair and tried to digest what had happened. The young woman somehow seemed to know me from somewhere. The older woman I'd try to trace by going through my old, dormant, medical files. That scar on the face that I made note of at the time, may help to trace her. Despite the neighbourhood both women did not seem to be in need.

The blonde young woman had said just before I left that she lived upstairs in the same building she was standing in front of. She had mentioned that she had a baby with her. Alva, as her name was, told me I need only pull the string dangling down from the second-floor window. That way a bell would sound and she would know someone was calling on her. She sounded like she didn't like missing calls. That was more than a lot of girls of her ilk could say. But her baby stuck in my mind. She had mentioned that it was only two weeks old. Yet she didn't strike me as a woman who had given birth recently.

I would go back soon after some think time to investigate the disappearance of the brother Ralph. I should try the police first but Holmes rarely did so when an investigation was underway and therefore I decided not to as well. Instead, I broke out thirteen cardboard cases full of old medical files collected during the years I practiced full time and also three years practicing part time. I was not that busy with Holmes those first years of our budding friendship before I moved up to his full time assistant. Shortly thereafter I closed my medical practice.

I looked through the files all-night and started again mid-morning. At twenty minutes before lunch I finally made a find.

It was then that our housekeeper walked in. She said, "You look like the winner of the sweepstakes."

I replied, "You're close and I hate to ask but can you make me a fresh cup of tea? I need an influx of energy. I must soon go out for a few hours."

"I certainly will, Dr. Watson, but where perchance are you going?"

"To try and clear up a twenty year old misunderstanding, and see what else I can uncover."

"Have your lunch first," my housekeeper said.

According to my files and thanks to the scar I had made note of years ago, I was now aware that the older of the two women was named Odelle Puddicome. The young blonde's last name was also Puddicome. Mother and daughter, I presumed.

The mother's boyfriend's name was Opal Shavi, a name that ended up in my files because apparently this Shavi had done time in an East Indian prison and also spent time in a penitentiary in Shanghai, China.

After lunch, it took twenty minutes to cover the distance from Baker Street where Holmes and I had lived for some years to the old neighbourhood and the excitement it brought.

It was time to ask questions of this Alva woman, perhaps hard questions to answer and whoever else I could find who may know something about this Puddicome bunch.

Firstly on arriving, however, I aimed directly at Bobbing's Laundry where Alva's brother had worked till recently. If nothing else, he would make a good alibi for a visit to this young Puddicome woman.

Mr. Bobbing spoke to me personally and he was very informative. One matter he cleared up was that this Opal Shavi was living with Odelle Puddicome almost like they were husband and wife. Bobbing went on to say that Odelle even used Shavi as her last name whenever she felt she could get away with it. Somehow the two had bonded to each other and lived together in a marriage of convenience. I led the discussion in the direction of Ralph.

Bobbing said, "To tell you a truthful story, Ralph has not gone very far. His girlfriend Eve could add on more details than I could. He had been up to something. What?, I do not know."

"I see. About this religion of hers, could the Salvation Army be involved in anything peculiar that may have led to

Ralph's sudden disappearance."

Bobbing replied, "I am sure he's alright, not that his family gives a damn."

I replied, "I know of his blonde sister, blonde for now at least. She, at our last meeting, did express great concern for her missing brother.

"Yes, and the mother is cut from the same cloth. They even look similar. If you should get a look at the mother you'll see the same lips, and nose, and you will see there is a family resemblance. The daughter's eyes are a dark brown and her hair naturally thanks to an Indian father, is black and thick.

"I see but what about the father who is also the husband of Odelle, husband of sorts, one could say?"."

Mr. Bobbing replied, "Now there's a piece of work. He's mainly East Indian but I hear one grandparent was English. He was in trouble with the law for years till eight, ten, years ago, when he started to seriously prosper. Whatever his occupation, it has started to pay big dividends.

I don't know what racket he's in but one reason why Ralph could have disappeared was he was not interested in joining his father's line of work. If Ralph knew too much, then perhaps the father had menaced him."

I said, "I can only presume then that this Ralph must not be criminally inclined."

"He is not, and I made note of his clear, untroubled mind. I found his conversation and insight more intelligent than average for whatever that may mean to those who may know of him.

I asked, "What if anything have the police done about this problem? I can only speculate, I am on my own. Yet perhaps they at least may know what racket this Shavi fellow is involved in that brings him such a lot of money. You have been very helpful. Is there anything else that might help me find Puddicome?"

Bobbing by nature outgoing, and backed by his successful business went on. "You may be aware of Opal Shavi's lengthy crime record. During his four years in a Calcutta prison one of his cellmates was a Wolfgang Hitler Matti. He taught Opal about body culture as a means of changing your physique as per desired. Women included. This Wolfgang was originally from Stuttgart."

I interrupted, "Keep going is there more to this

relationship?"

"Yes. Shavi was given a short term in a prison in Shanghai, China. He was dealing in drugs and a lot of Chinese people were using drugs. That's why such a short sentence I would say."

While in prison he also learned how to mesmerize people with his oratorical skills and how to hypnotize willing participants. The two prisons provided him with an unusual education. He learned the tools of his current trade. He knows how to clinch a deal and get paid well. But what racket is it, I suspect prostitution but perhaps not. It may go deeper.

Since then he was arrested twice here in Britain. Once he got off, the second time he did three years. Since then he lived a pretty good lifestyle."

I remarked, "Well, that's about it I suppose."

"Pretty well," Bobbing said, "Although there is one more small detail. Over the last few years I had seen Opal Shavi speaking at different times to three pregnant women. Now it is almost like he is above the law but that may soon change."

Bobbing had a wealth of knowledge. The criminal faction in this area respected him. He was a kind man and he kept his eyes and ears open. It wasn't unusual for him to find a job for a needy relative of certain criminals. But he did have a loose tongue.

Now all I needed to find out was the racket these women seemed to be involved in with Opal as the ringleader. Bobbing told me that Opal was in contact with three other women besides his relatives. All women, according to Bobbing, were of ill repute. Their behaviour was far too seedy to be typical working class female behaviour; and despite no job they were dressed well enough and the young one Alva, the daughter of Odelle had her own small apartment. Something was off the mark here somewhere. It would take a good-sized effort to unravel these relationships.

After talking to Bobbing, I went directly to the apartment of Alva, the young blonde woman. This time I could see her coal black roots showing. It turned out to be more of a bedsitting room than an apartment.

When Alva met me at the door she said, "Ordinarily I wouldn't let you in but there is someone here who wants to talk to you."

I walked in to the sound of a shrieking baby. The room

conditions were pitiful; it felt like an abusive situation. Shavi must be pocketing most of the take.

After my eyes became focused I looked at the chair near the baby's crib. Sitting there was Odelle. Yes, I was now sure that both were blood relatives. She looked at me with a surly grimace on her face.

I said, "Hello."

The woman I treated close to twenty years ago, had the same tell-tale scar on her face. She had wanted treatment for a sexually transmitted disease of the common variety. At that time, she was a hard-bitten woman and very argumentative.

She asked, "Do you ever think of righting the wrong you did to me?"

I asked in return, "What wrong pray tell? I'm sure whatever the prescription I gave you at the time was all you needed. There is no outright cure."

I remembered that a few months after her first visit to my office she came back and accused me of getting her pregnant. Apparently, the baby was going to be born out of wedlock because her boyfriend didn't believe in marriage. That could cause difficulties for this Puddicome woman. She needed a man she could fall back on. It was all just a ruse on her part and not a very clever one. Intelligence was not her gift. I did her no wrong.

As I looked about the dingy room she started in all over again.

"You ruined my name and there is our daughter. You owe me satisfaction. After I undressed, you immediately became infatuated with my cleavage. You, Doctor, took advantage of me."

"Ludicrous," I replied. "Quite impossible."

She stated, "Either give me fifty pounds or I'll go to the police."

I declared, "They wouldn't be at all interested."

There was something about this woman that gave her warped views on her pregnancy a personally disturbing situation for me to be in. Coupled with the fact the ignored infant was still crying, put me on edge. It was a child that Alva obviously did not care for.

The older Puddicome woman was coming to her senses. She wasn't quite seething as she was before. Her facial features registered her disdain however.

She continued, "If you don't give me satisfaction I will have my husband speak to you and he is a man of violence. It will leave you ruined."

I replied, "Not interested."

My working hypothesis is that Opal Shavi learned hypnotism in the penitentiary and used it on women to make it easier for him to convince these women to carry their illegitimate children. It had to be for the black market in babies. I still wasn't fully convinced of it but it was the most obvious reason.

Odelle bellowed, "Get the hell out." As I walked away I thought I had heard a few other choice words.

I spoke to Alva; "I will come back tomorrow hopefully with good news on your brother. Try to be alone."

She said, "I will pay you as much as I can as I hate to give money to my own father."

I replied, "If there ever comes a need I could prove medically that I am not your blood relative."

I had soon hailed a hansom for home. I asked the driver

to stop by a newsstand where I bought a copy of the London Daily Express.

I could use some reading to fill my evening as my lifelong friend Holmes should soon be as fit as ever.

On digesting my new information, I should break the investigative mould and ask the police for help in the case.

In the meantime, I wondered if perhaps this Alva had developed a father fixation on me. I may well be replacing her real father but I think Alva had passed that stage and instead wanted to practice violence on men.

After supper and tea, I took a second cup into the study with me. I was looking forward to enjoying the newspaper. After an hour or so and my tea all gone, I was ready to put the paper aside when I came across a small passage all of three paragraphs long.

The column was entitled, "Black Market Babies Shame." My interest was piqued. For whatever reason my stomach was feeling hollow and I felt a bit depressed. Well, agitated anyway, I read the article, with anxiety taking hold of me.

The story read, "The only good news is the police are aware of this heinous crime and they have a few leads. It seems to be partly located in North East London, a district of the city that has fallen on hard times this past decade. The streets there are often unsafe."

I realized that they were talking of my old neighbourhood. I left the district permanently, about 18 years ago. To add a footnote to the existentialist philosophy, this world will not end until all has been seen and done, and all have lived who were meant to live.

There was the fixation by both women on blaming me for getting Odelle Puddicome pregnant. Then there was the crying baby that judging from the smell permeating from Alva's place was being shockingly neglected, not even the child's diaper looked after. I had best call the police.

The police officer on the phone and I talked at some length. I was connected to him because he was one of two sergeants working on the black market for babies.

His name was Alf Meadows. I told him what I knew and that I was planning on confronting Alva with my accusation tomorrow afternoon.

He firmly stated, "I suggest you wait till early tomorrow evening about seven. We can get there by then and you may need to be supported. It is best if you wait for us.

I asked, "What makes you want to help?"

Sergeant Meadows said, "You arrived at the same conclusion we did. We did have circumstantial evidence at first but it would only take a few simple tests to strengthen the evidence to above circumstantial. Besides the two females you indicated, we know of three more and they will be rounded up by another police squad at the same time."

I replied, "This Odelle Puddicome also accused me of being the father of her daughter. No such thing is true."

Sergeant Meadows replied, "As for the same Puddicome, she uses Shavi for her last name when she feels it's safe. The husband did time with a German in an Indian prison where Shavi is originally from. As a result of the British Empire connection Shavi was allowed to waltz right into England without any roadblocks. The German cellmate had a strong influence on him. His name is Wolfgang Hitler Matti. He was masterful in matters of a dark nature. He was viewed as a troublemaker by the prison authorities and was an influence on Shavi.

I asked, "About this Opal Shavi then, all in all, what

insight can you offer?"

The sergeant replied, "We think he is one of the gang leaders if not in complete control. We are concerned that he is the head of the criminal ring selling the black-market babies.

Three days ago, out of the blue, strong evidence reached us. Ralph Puddicome, son of Odelle and brother to Alva Puddicome, came into police headquarters and told us everything we need to know of the entire racket; names, locations, even the names of a few people who bought the babies. The case against the women and Opal Shavi looks strong. Ralph betrayed the gang but only because they deserved it. Join us at Alva Puddicome's address as we planned to arrive unannounced at 7:00 p.m. Then we go in. Four of us will be arriving in Daimler autocars and two more will come in on horseback and two more horses will be drawing a van that we can lock the suspects in."

I asked, "Getting back to Ralph what made him do it?" The Sergeant replied, "He said that he hoped God made note of it. The police, in the meantime have offered a reward so he will end up with a good deal of cash. God can be slow in acting."

"My Lord as it were, talk about a break," I declared.

The sergeant Alf Meadows said in reply, "I have been delighted ever since. He is a decent enough young fellow." I had a quiet evening and went up to check on the detectives progress. It should not be long. He was even eating better. The next day passed quickly.

Soon it was 6:30 p.m. and I hailed a hansom. I gave him the directions very carefully. I arrived at six-fifty and waited patiently for the police. They were scheduled to show up at about seven p.m. It was an important case so they should be prompt.

It was now two minutes to seven and still no police. I heard the second-floor window open. It was Alva. She said, "Have you been there long?"

"No, just a couple of minutes."

"Why not tell me Dr. Watson?"

"I was afraid your mother might be with you."

Alva replied, "No, she's not due for another half an hour. I'd really like news on Ralph of any kind."

"On asking," "I replied, "everyone seems to feel he is fine."

"I do not see why you do not come up then. I'm going out as soon as mother arrives and we will be gone for a while."

I replied, "I see." I looked at my watch and it was just at seven. I added, "Yes, I suppose I will come up." If I had to I would collar her myself.

She came down and opened the door. Then she went up.

I decided to take one more chance. I took out the clipping I had culled from the newspaper on the black-market babies and placed it in the doorjamb just above the keyhole. The police, if they did find it, would know it was I. How late were they going to be? Alva's mother was due here soon. If she came first, my life would be in great danger.

As soon as I went upstairs and was let in to her bedsitting room I could see the baby without any blanket on him. It wasn't that cold, but still inappropriate.

I was going to launch into my fictionalized Ralph story when she started in on her fixation that was me as her biological father. I think somehow I fit a close enough psychological description of her idea of a father. But then her mind was deranged. My denial of any shared ancestry left her hating me.

I looked at her sitting on the bed made up with cheap

blankets and I wondered what next was to happen. Still, no police. Did I get the time right? Hopefully!

She said, "So I am not good enough for you then?"

I replied, "You are mistaken and I am not your father."

She remarked, "I don't really care, father or otherwise, I loathe you. And you no doubt in your conceit thought I loved you and must have you as my father. As you can see you are wrong." Then she pulled out a revolver from her bag that she had left lying on the bed where she sat. The gun was pointed directly at me. It looked like an American made colt revolver. She had somehow procured one.

I said, "Why don't you hear me out. I know you are a wronged woman. I have no doubt that your father Opal Shavi must have done you harm." If only she would transfer her anger to where it belonged. It was the only weapon I had.

I was suspicious that Opal Shavi had molested her. That way she could have turned to strange violent behaviour. Even children were included.

But my death was only moments away when I heard voices in the hall outside her door. I heard the welcome sound of police boots stomping on her hallway floor. A voice from the hallway shouted, "Open up, police!"

I was not sure what would happen next but she threw the gun to the floor, opened the window and was part way out. The police burst through the door with one blow, she could not move. Apparently, she had snagged her sweater on a nail sticking out of the windowsill. In addition, her large cleavage kept her stuck in the small window frame. The arrest was soon made and I was quite relieved.

The other women and Odelle were soon rounded up as was Opal and Opal's assistant, known to the police but not to me. The reason for the delay was one of the police cars had malfunctioned but was soon revived.

I was given a lift down to the police station where I saw the four women being locked in the same cell and the same treatment for the two men. Odelle had not been pregnant in some time and kept both children. She was shown to another cell and was charged with being a material witness. After a chat then came "an against" regulations drink or two after which a young constable drove me right to my door. It was nice to be home.

Holmes would be fully recovered in a day or two and I

was quite pleased with the story I would be able to share. The lowly assistant to the great Sherlock Holmes was a capable sleuth in his own right.

A Subdued Affair

It was a subdued affair, but then my friend of longstanding, the celebrated detective Sherlock Holmes, was celebrating his retirement. He looked well. As his Physician Dr. Watson, now retiring as well, I was one of the guests at the party. For many years now, wherever Holmes went, I followed. More than one of my patients could attest to that. My medical career was close to shambles, from my first meeting with Holmes many years ago, until our retirement.

I had become well known from early on, through my association with the superlative detective. I contributed to his success, as best I could, but my abilities compared to his were virtually always of a secondary nature. Some of his more interesting cases, I chronicled in written form, as the years went by, much to the delight of more than one publisher and avid readers everywhere.

The reason for his retirement was he claimed that

He wasn't quite as nimble as before, and that his immense mental faculties had slowed, but not much more than a trifle. I could vouch for that. I was a few years his junior and my years had caught up to me, as well.

For the last brief while we had been looked after by our new domestic, Hughena Hillier. We recently had procured the service of a young jack of all trades Michael Brennan. He did what Hughena was not physically capable of doing.

He was third generation Irish and doing better than the masses that came over to seek the construction jobs available when Holmes and I were still children at home with our families.

Hughena had helped Holmes with his grooming to prepare him for the festive affair at hand. He'd napped just after his wash and appeared quite energetic.

I looked at my friend of many years, and considering what we had gone through during our career I felt satisfied. He, the Detective and I, his assistant had both weathered the storm worn years of our lives well enough. On too many occasions we had both found ourselves under the most harrowing of circumstances. More than once our lives were at stake.

Tea was being poured by young Hughena for all, except for a few well wishers who wanted only to extend their congratulations and with all due courtesy, left our gathering shortly after. Even the councilman for our district, had dropped by to wish Holmes a happy retirement, only to depart shortly after. He had garnered a vote or two for himself while here, I daresay. Holmes, running true to course, lit up one of his infrequent smokes. Holmes had cut back on his tobacco habit, on the advice of a surprisingly young doctor. It was duly noted that this young doctor exercised more influence than I could ever bring to bear on Holmes. But then, he and I had never made a fuss over any of our differences.

As I looked discreetly about our comfortable, well furbished sitting room, used for the occasion, there was a peaceful hum of best wishes, light laughter, and words of praise, all in honour of the occasion of our friend as he said goodbye to a most fruitful career. He had been a marvel. As for me a lot of the ambience of the moment reflected its glow on me. There were those who said their goodbyes to me as well. I was most contented because I had been recognized by one and all as a man deserving to bask in the warm glow of the afternoon's festivities. Being older does bring an array of blessings.

It was but three p.m. when the pace of the party seemed to decline slightly. That was soon changed when Inspector Hartigan, the successor to Inspector Lestrade, who had arrived later than most, had one more honour to bestow on one of the world's most brilliant investigative minds.

In the inspector's possession, was a certificate of high merit from Scotland Yard for my dear friend, Sherlock Holmes, to thank him and to praise him for his help in solving many cases over the years. The award was to double as a retirement present.

One of the invited guests a friend of our MP walked up to Holmes and said, "Detective Holmes, not all of us ever saw your brilliant mind at work in person. Is there perhaps a way you could talk at some length of one of your lesser known cases and how you solved it."

Holmes said, "I was just thinking of such a case a few days ago, when I was having trouble sleeping. Even the press did not quite jump on board. It was scandalous what happened."

A brother of the Anglican deacon asked, "Can you elaborate on what must have happened?"

"I can and will" Holmes replied.

"It all started with the embezzlement of one hundred and sixty thousand pounds from a British Bank. The crook turned out to be one of their own accountants. To complicate matters he also murdered his girlfriend. She knew too much.

I soon recovered the money and not long afterwards I solved the murder of his girlfriend. The wretched crooks name is Willard Tyler.

The thief turned murderer received his final denouement from me and my dedicated pursuit. I did not give up until the successful conclusion of the case. Mr. Trainor asked, once again, "Did you have good help?"

Holmes replied, "Well of course there was Dr. Watson but in the end it came down to me and Bob Twiggs. This Bob Twiggs, was a London cab driver and the son of Billie Twiggs, one of Watson's and my own favourite hansom operators, who had delivered us safely, back home to Baker Street, after more than one hair—raising escapade. Ask Watson, he will soon tell you." Then Holmes turned his attention to his tea.

When I took over Holmes first contacted Bob Twiggs, young Bob immediately recognized the name, and could hardly wait to shuttle Holmes about, in the pursuit of one more victory over the criminal element. I remember this case well. It was all so sordid it is hard for me to recount it all. However it was interesting to relive that sordid mess. I shall try to recite what I can since we are all in agreement to hear about one of my less famous triumphs over crime. You may see my essence in what you are going to hear."

The murderer was a bank accountant and therefore the theft was a considerable amount of money. His method, he being Willard Tyler, was to deliberately reduce the addition of certain amounts of money entering the bank's system through accounts receivable and as such became deposited in the bank. He manipulated the false amounts of cash in such a way that every week during that particular business quarter he walked out of the bank with a packet of stolen bank notes. There are three months in a business quarter and after that Tyler knew that if he didn't run and hide, then he would likely be arrested. The bank audits all their business accounts every three months. His covert banking irregularities had a very short lifespan, but he was prepared for the end result of this foul deed.

Then came a serious crimp in his plans. For reasons known to the bank, and because the bank president was soon retiring and the new man was already chosen, the new head wanted a full accounting of the books, before he took charge of the bank. He had asked for a thorough review of the bank's quarterly statement six days earlier than originally scheduled.

Those numbers he would attribute to his predecessor's reign, those following, to his own. At the completion of the audit, the bank was to go back to its regular routine. The new president wanted to develop a clear understanding of current business practices within the bank.

This upset the skilfully arranged plans of the bank embezzler and he had to disappear from the bank close to a week earlier than scheduled.

Willard Tyler needed a new plan, but it would have to be one put together in a hurry. There was much to do, and all of it under the cover of secrecy, and away from the eyes of the law. Soon they would be on to him but he felt as though he could avoid detection until he soon left the country. His ship would be sailing in another week. Without knowing it at the time, this delay gave me time to pursue the case at hand and make my deductions.

After the story came out, including the story of the murder of the crook's girlfriend by the aforementioned embezzler, the BBC radio and the daily papers carried all available information. I wondered till near the end if some of this foul deed would be suppressed, but it was not.

Apparently, before Tyler murdered his girlfriend they had gotten into an argument. The stress of criminal activity took its toll on the couple. The apartment walls were thin and people could hear bits and pieces of the rather loud argument. Holmes could easily see the underlying undercurrents between the theft and the murder immediately. Tyler had obviously told the girlfriend too much while drunk. He immediately saw the danger and killed her to shut her up. Liquor was just one of his weaknesses. He consumed it in large quantities. Indolence was another.

Dr. Watson joined the story telling.

Because of all this preliminary information, Holmes had a head start. Helping the police find the murder weapon, one could say, was but one more candle on his retirement cake.

Hughena asked, "Do you mean Dr. Watson that he had practically had it solved already?"

I replied, "What you do not know is that the retiring detective has incredible powers of deduction. A few scraps of information was all he needed quite often." Hughena replied, "And he is hardly any bother at all much like you."

I said, "Another noteworthy matter I must share with you

people, and our young friend, is a letter arrived yesterday addressed to Detective Sherlock Holmes from one of Europe's crowned heads."

On opening the letter a little earlier, I was aware it contained best retirement wishes from the King of Bohemia, a royal personage Holmes and I were of some service as called upon. What a case that was, and so charming of the King to remember our service after all this time. Hughena smiled as I read the warm wishes from the King, enclosed in the card. To Holmes and I, it brought back poignant memories, especially of Irene Alder. She was a woman that Holmes respected. There was a valid reason for Holme's high regard for her.

Inspector Hartigan asked, "Please, if I may Detective, getting back to the case at hand, how did you manage to so much as get your feet wet in such an investigation?"

Holmes replied, "When the bank asked me to investigate for them, I could hardly wait. It was the murder of his girlfriend that turned out to make the case. That murder helped enlighten me early on. The theft and murder fit together like hand and glove. It was the murder victim's mother who first enlightened me enough to consider the small, but helpful, body of evidence as worth examining more fully. The police were more neutral than anything else. From there I but followed my instincts or 'gut feelings' one could say. I mean that more literally than figuratively, Inspector. There was much information that reached me by the way of excellent newspaper accounts and the thorough news announcers on the BBC radio. It was mainly the local London Town news report on the hour that I waited for. The story, as you know, spread nationwide so there was no shortage of coverage, at times in the most minute of detail.

Some wanted this matter hushed up out of respect for a family that this Willard Tyler was related to. Willard was soon disowned by them."

"Well I will be."

I remarked to Holmes, "But the money, quite often isn't recovered. You not only found the full amount, but it was found hidden away in a valise with Tyler's own private monogram on it. That helped convince the jury. It also made an opportune getaway impossible."

Holmes replied, "Again the victim's mother, she was a fount of information early on. During a series of interviews by professional news reporters especially the first few days immediately following this tragic incident, she gave her account of the murder and spared none of even the most minor details of the homicide so close to her home and heart. Her first-hand commentary included a description of the murderer's condition at the time."

I asked, "Would this perhaps be her way of trying to aid the police in their pursuit of the interloper"? I was not that active in the ongoing details of the case."

Holmes replied, "My dear Watson, you're not far wrong, but barring some of these new-fangled psychiatrists and psychologists coming to your aid you've just barely passed first year detective school on this matter. Apparently, there is such a thing now as a 'detective school'. The mother found talking about the murder a catharsis that helped soothe her troubled emotions."

Inspector Hartigan, chuckling, said "You and I both".

Holmes replied, "The afternoon is young yet. As for the crooked accountant, he had the opportunity and the motive. The motive being the life of ease and luxury, the bank's money would buy him. He, from what I could gather, wasn't much more than a drunkard who used women of easy virtue. As for the murder, again, he had a motive but no opportunity. The more successful murderers plan the act in advance. Willard Tyler was caught, not quite in the act, but in the cover up. As for the theft, he used the bank as the means for his opportunity."

"I risk sounding pretentious here, but to some extent, and I've studied this matter at some length, there is no such thing as non-premeditated murder. Then again, this Tyler man was very drunk and he was also quite frustrated. The bank had just put a huge dent in his plans.

I looked over at Holmes and he was still enjoying himself. The extra effort of story telling gave him a good energy and he carried on.

"One frustration was that Tyler missed the chance to steal another large sum of currency. He wanted it all. To make matters worse, in his drunken, perhaps partially insane frame of mind, he couldn't think straight. When he gave his girlfriend too much information about this nefarious deed of his and at the time, not quite capable of thinking clearly, the simple solution was to kill this young Noreen Boutilier. It may only have taken him a few moments to decide to murder the poor woman, but by my standards that was enough thought to make the murder a planned killing, premeditated, in other words." Hartigan entered, "Instead Detective, I would hardly call a few moments as premeditation."

Holmes replied, "Once the murder act is decided on, there is no law that says he has to philosophize on the sordid enough act as it is.

Instead, he would run towards the light. The light has always been safer. It was like a statement of innocence to him. It was an attempt to cleanse his conscience.

I checked and saw where there was a brightly lit fish and chips wagon not far from this Boutilier woman's apartment. Next to the chip wagon was a billiard academy, it as well, with outside lighting."

The reason why this was so important was I know that this sorry excuse for a man would want to hide the murder weapon and as soon as possible. It was his way of cleansing himself, that and his mind had slowly gone out of control from the strain of his emotions and matters pertaining to his crime going against him. I informed the police of the huge metal bucket behind the fish and chips wagon, I had reconnoitred, and it was full of potato peelings and fish scraps. I strongly suspected that they would find the murder weapon there.

This Willard Tyler was frightened and acting

irrationally. He felt overly encumbered by this strange turn of fate. He remained rattled throughout this entire incident. He was sobering up by that time and had sense enough to know he may be in trouble.

The inspector interceded briefly and said, "You performed a great victory for jurisprudence. It all went that much better because of your effort."

I looked at the inspector, and then at Holmes, as he raised his teacup to his lips. I asked of Hughena, "Please, dear woman more tea, and soon".

"Immediately", she replied.

I quickly addressed my old friend of many years. I said, "If it's not too much to ask of you young man... "

"Cease," interrupted Holmes, "now state your case."

I replied, "It would make a fitting climax for our delightful afternoon's affair if you were to grant the Inspector's wish."

Holmes replied, "I shall be only too happy to do so, but the tea and more to come, you see, makes a visit to the lavatory the first order of the day."

Then came the tea.

The inspector addressed me, "Watson dear fellow, have I asked too much of your friend? Am I straining his faculties?"

I replied, "Not at all. He has had a nap and he is quite vigorous yet. He is very alert."

Mrs. Hudson, she herself looking tired, spoke up. "I can vouch for that Inspector. It was only a year or two ago when he would be on the tear all day and into the evening if it were needed. There was no day of rest for the detective and his fully capable partner."

Holmes was soon back and immediately set in on the task at hand of unravelling this chain of sordid events that led to the solving of this case to everyone's satisfaction. Imminent now, was the presentation of a Certificate of Merit, from Scotland Yard. One more honour for this esteemed gentleman.

Holmes cleared his throat and quickly swallowed a drop or two of tea. Then he said, "Ordinarily there would have been no involvement on my part in this matter, I will just mention that the bank was soon in touch with me immediately after Willard did not show up that first day for work. By a fluke chance his carefully laid plans went awry.

Holmes continued to grant their wish. He commenced, "After the murder, the victim's mother, the Boutilier woman, was interviewed by a couple of reporters from two of the local daily newspapers. Each reporter outdid himself trying to pry loose the whole story. That body of information was a major assist to what soon became my part in solving this shameful affair. Again, I just followed my nose."

"The victim's mother described the scene of the murder in such vivid detail, that I soon had enough clues to proceed tentatively into the heart of the matter within the second morning after the fact. It didn't take long. About the recovered money, I found out early that the money had been previously buried that was a major interest to me. The bank had asked me to try to recover the money. You might say I was soon involved up to my ears. Why not, the first news story gave me enough ammunition to fire up my powers of deduction. Shortly after I had more than an inkling, a solid starting point, as you can understand.

The first round of information gave me what was an approximate idea of where to search for the missing funds. It was a start. The money had obviously been buried before the slaying. That was indirectly caused by a problem that developed concerning his transportation out of the country. But that is another part of the story.

"Of course, Tyler's native intelligence, not being terribly anaemic, spelled out his need for a hideout. The banks rescheduling had thrown a monkey wrench into his plans. He also needed another place for the cash. If that were found on him, if the law didn't catch up with him, then the underworld would. I have no doubt the original plan included leaving the country, but he had mistimed his exit."

"The murder victim's mother, Anne Boutilier, talked freely and openly about the murder of her daughter Noreen. She also described the murderer, his condition, and his actions, and talked openly about the site of the actual murder describing it well. This information I found invaluable to me. It was a valid start. With no qualms whatsoever, I placed this Tyler monstrosity at the location of the murder. That alone could get him to trial but a good lawyer could reduce the evidence to circumstantial. To be sure of a conviction I needed more proof and with more substance to it. At least the legal authorities had a corpse. Then there was his embezzlement charge. That alone meant a prison sentence.

"I soon went to work. I found this Tyler's actions intolerable, and yet he somehow, appearance wise, reminded me of someone I knew."

"The weapon was believed to be a knife belonging to the victim. It had gone missing, but I had a careful description of it. Where was the knife at now?"

"Tyler was reported to be drunk and bellicose at the time of the murder. The drunken part made it a bit simpler to track down the hidden cash. The mother's information throughout was invaluable. As for the murder weapon, I soon sent the police off in the right direction."

"That much was based on a supposition of mine that I had observed in some of my cases, throughout the years. Some murderers are attracted to light but not until after the deed is done."

"This Willard Tyler was tall and obese. Drunk as he was, he slowly stomped up the staircase to his girlfriend's second floor apartment. Because he was so heavy footed he dislodged a lot of the muck from his boots. It had been raining in London that day. He had to stop at the second-floor landing to catch his breath. Despite being only in his thirties, he had already gone to seed.

As it turned out he was a son of one of the prominent British families. 'Formerly was' would be more appropriate. His photograph that I'd seen in a couple of London Daily's gave that away. Instead of rising to the advantages of his birthright, he sank further, and further, into depravity. Women and liquor were among two of his vices. He liked to gamble as well, but not always heavily. That paired with a lack of ambition was how he lived his life.

Hartigan interrupted enough to say, "This is sheer brilliance. Others would have been stymied at finding out even half that much information."

Holmes replied, "There is nothing that brilliant about placing a phone call."

I remembered Holmes putting a call through to Sir Harry's private club that Holmes felt sure would impart some information, even in passing, on this Tyler wretch.

The inspector added, "It is amazing what you do."

I thought surely the Inspector was overdoing his flattery, but Holmes let it pass. This case was the usual result of Holme's expert sleuthing.

I stated, "I tell you inspector, he's barely scratched the surface of his involvement. My friend, you see inspector, has this analytic mind and is a very shrewd judge of character. He is rarely fooled, although both he and I remember, ruefully, a few that slipped through our well constructed traps."

"I see," replied Inspector Hartigan, "but please do continue."

Instead I replied, "Firstly inspector, don't forget the Yards fine work when they finally flushed Tyler out from the opium den. It was in the basement of the Chinaman's cafe, in one of London's most notorious districts. Another two and half days without the Yard, and he may have successfully skipped the country. If one facet of a case changes, often other theories and assumptions are affected as well. The world at large is full of such "ifs" in plenteous abundance."

I studied Holmes's countenance when I spoke. Rather than tiring he was becoming more and more animated. For now, he was smiling and showing his still healthy teeth. He had a wrinkle. Yet here I was with my slight paunch. Not to be outdone by Holmes, my hair was thinning as well. The problem was Holmes had started out with a more plentiful crop than my own.

The fresh tea had arrived, and Holmes had barely sampled his steaming cup full, before he sallied forth.

"At the murder scene, both mother and daughter lived on the second floor, but in different apartments. Thanks to Mrs. Boutilier, I soon found out that Tyler had tracked in some dark mud. Tyler was the only visitor that day. The building was usually quiet and the weather made it more so. It had been raining. His footsteps were heavy to begin with and coated in a black mud with traces of sand in the mud. A tree leaf was included in this mixture of elements. The mud mixture could potentially be a help in finding the money. But where would you find black mud, and with loose sand being present even that may not be enough. I presumed the wind had blown the leaf free of its branch, either way, for whatever reason, other than an eager radio man wanting as much detail as possible, I had the leaf described to me via the air waves. On listening it was, I presumed, a leaf from a chestnut tree. They are quite common and are different from trees even whose foliage is similar. For example, the leaf itself is a little coarser to the touch than a lot of other tree leaves. The sand could mean that there was a construction site nearby. That helped considerably. There had been sand mixed in with the mud and because my embezzlement suspect was now a murder suspect I could easily see the beauty of investigating the murder as well and all it entailed.

Holmes paused for one sip of tea followed by a more robust second taste. I could tell he enjoyed Hughena's tea. I fancied it myself.

Hughena spoke right up. I could tell she was finally starting to feel at home here on Baker Street. She said then there is Mr. Holmes' impeccable reputation that stood him in good stead, when he somehow contacted Bob, the son of the retired hansom driver, the same driver known well to Mr. Holmes and his assistant Doctor Watson. Because of that, Bob, if you'll pardon the pun, went the extra mile for the hopefully, now fully retired, detective. You all must pardon me for going on and on, but I have a slightly older person or two that I enjoy taking care of, and very much so."

The finding of the murder weapon brought sadness over me. Noreen Boutilier most likely had used the same knife to dissect a chicken, or prepare a ham for the oven."

"I feel as though I must tell you of another fond memory recently awakened in my being. I feel almost compelled to tell you all". Today, my only boyhood friend, Harry Mould, wired me. It has been fifty years since we parted company, for the last time."

"My home, yes, yes..." The detective stopped in midstream. He looked wistful. There had been a mess.

Hughena came to the rescue and said, "Try the tea Holmes dear, you'll find it comforting, and more than a tiny sip or two."

Holmes did so, composed himself briefly and continued, "The whole place, the home I had lived in crashed downward, landing on my sore, frustrated plate. I was then sent off to school, a comfortable distance away from my parents and that tragic incident. My friend Harry, I never heard from again, until today. Well yesterday actually. Our last contact was fifty years ago. He apparently recognized me, through a photograph of me, in one of the local papers concerning my retirement. Thence the telegram, once he confirmed my identity."

Holmes dug into his reserves and continued. I decided not to mention a quick look I had taken at the telegram where I noticed a question mark after the name Sherlock Holmes. But Holmes did express his satisfaction with the telegram.

He said, "I suppose, in a way, it was like I received a little extra dollop of icing on my not quite fully demolished cake."

"As it turned out, the wretched renegade, Willard Tyler had a very influential father, I shall touch on briefly, by the name of Sir Harry Tyler, a multi millionaire, and an OBE to boot.

I was satisfied somehow, but in a peculiar fashion, Sir Harry handled the matter thoroughly the only possible way he could. He made not the slightest attempt to influence the courts. He didn't even try to find him a good lawyer. Instead, an advertisement appeared in a London daily newspaper and the personal column of a popular tabloid publication, where Sir Harry publicly disowned this Tyler character."

Inspector Hartigan added, "Merely conjecture on my part Detective Holmes, but would I be right in saying that the reason why your boyhood friends and acquaintances, perhaps others as well, rarely contacted you is because you may have changed your name at some previous time. I'm sure there were more people in your life at that time, than young Mr. Mould."

Holmes' eyebrows rose perceptfully and he said, "It's not a foreign thought to me Inspector."

The Inspector's left shoulder dropped as Hartigan shifted a bit to his left side.

Holmes continued, "I once thought of it when I was a troubled young man. The second, and last time was for security reasons only. My life had been threatened by the Tongs, a vicious Russian mob with considerable influence in the orient."

"I see."

The Inspector's head shifted downward, and I saw where the crown of his head had a pronounced bald spot. He was a husky man but not tall. Unlike Inspector Lestrade, he had no obvious facial hair, but was clean shaven.

Holmes delved deeper and straight ahead, "I have more on the continuing saga of Sir Harry Tyler. The true Harry, as he once was."

I interrupted Holmes, "Hopefully old friend, with nothing less than kindness. Lest we forget Sir Harry is an OBE."

Holmes replied, "Yes, but I daresay, Sir Harry, under the circumstances, would easily understand. Our motives are of a benign, concerned nature, after all. And we meant him no ill will. Not only that, but word reached me from my old friend, Henry Gibbons, that Sir Harry was soon to leave the country. The reason why he had chosen Canada is royal titles of any kind, are not welcome there, well at least officially not welcome, and therefore should not be used, no matter what the title. While Canada is a part of the British Empire, despite that, his shame need never be known. His plans were not quite definite but it was certain he would be leaving, if he had not done so already. I say Watson, you can understand what I'm trying to impart here, is that not so? The story everyone wants."

I remarked, "Indeed, I am enlightened enough Holmes, but Sir Harry, before this sordid odd thing came to be had his heart set on making one last fortune, he was about to buy a hefty sized coal deposit somewhere in North East England. Four hundred million tons of still unmined coal and the price was reasonable enough. As for the price of coal in commodity form, it was appreciating in value on the world markets. A shortage of coal in Russia is adding to the upward pressure of the price per ton. Poor Sir Harry had his heart broken. They say if the deal had gone through Sir Harry would have been the richest man in England."

Holmes mentioned, "Before that the scandal was kept repressed decently enough. Not much was ever said."

Holmes added, "A point worth noting was Sir Harry had not been at his club since the incident first came to light. A rushed exit could have easily been made to some other country and for the best. Still his own flesh and blood had been arrested in a London slum, hiding in the Chinaman's Cafe, a place where opium is sold and imbibed in and many other criminal acts as well."

"Remarkably this odd character, very strange really, considering his family background, was soon to leave the country and by then, of course, with a few days to spare before the authorities knew the full story. Recovering the monogrammed valise full of money, with even Willard's middle initial on it, ensured a positive identification. This helped prove positively that he was the thief in question, therefore, the murderer. I knew I needed an extra pair of legs, so I hired young Bob Twiggs, and his motorized hansom, as I called it, to help transport me about. Hard evidence was still needed."

My first stop was to Noreen's home. Once I arrived and introduced myself, I was still well known at the time, I asked Mrs. Boutilier if I could look around. There was still a little mud on the steps and I could see traces of sand, none however of the leaf. From there I asked if I may look into Noreens apartment and permission was granted. After a brief look seeing nothing I came across an interesting curio.

On the way to the graveyard I said, "To think he killed her when he was drunk."

Bob replied, "And left behind some decent clues."

I said, the mud especially, a common product at gravesites. Once there look for black earth." It was a Saint Christopher medal. The front of the medal read, "Saint Christopher Safe Voyage." The obverse side had an inscription which read, "St. Mary's Graveyard." It had a little muck on it as well but not quite as dark as the muck on the stairway. I put two and two together and told Bob that we need now to find Saint Mary's Graveyard.

Bob Twiggs said, "We could go to the arch diocese of London office on Church Street."

I replied, "Yes they could help. So let us try."

But we were soon underway and found the diocesan office from which came directions to Saint Mary's Graveyard.

Holmes replied, "Yes, perhaps he had no plans to kill her, I continued, "Perhaps he had no plans to kill her but in his drunken state, he talked too freely about his fraudulent activities at the bank. He did not know whether that information was safe with her or not, so befuddled as he was, he chose to kill her. In his state, he presumed incorrectly he would get away with it."

"The fact that the bank may soon have been on to him as far as knew, but not how soon, and his passage out of England delayed due to an unavoidable miscalculation that he had made a few weeks earlier, before the bank had changed around their usual accounting procedures, caught Tyler by surprise. However, he did know that he would be safely out of sight at the Chinaman's cafe, but that his money wouldn't be safe on those premises. It was the murder that really ruined him. But the scales of Justice and the masterful British legal system came through and another murderer paid for his crimes."

Once Bob and I came to Saint Marys we both felt a connection at hand and went in past the gate. We walked straight ahead on well worn path, but there was no trace of black mud. On the corner was a construction site that may have provided the sand. It was a reason to continue our search.

After we walked for a few minutes I saw a pond with a

small walking bridge across it. It walked quickly in that direction and was soon on the shoreline of the pond.

Inspector Hartigan cleared his throat. I glanced his way and saw where his suit collar was bunched up higher than it should have been on his neck. He needed a better tailor. Still, he was used to being surrounded by subordinates instead of his present, more august company. His shoe wear may have been comfortable but the design of the shoe left something to be desired. Of course, he was, no doubt, on his feet considerably during the day and looking for comfort from a shoe rather than style.

The inspector asked, "Then the money had already been buried by the time he went to this Boutilier woman's place?"

Holmes replied, "Yes the clues left behind at the murder scene led to enough information for me to start an educated search for the money and once I had the money it led back to the murder scene and more proof that Willard was the murderer. If nothing much else there was the St. Christopher medal to consider.

But allow me continue. There from seven or eight feet to the right of the bridge was a small peat moss deposit left behind from before the graveyard extension when there was enough peat moss left for later harvesters to fertilize their gardens and to use for fuel. Other than here it was completely non-existent. My shoes were soon full of a black mud.

Bob provided me with a spade he kept in his tool kit and despite the mud I soon uncovered a leather valise and with Willards initials on it including his middle initial.

With Willard the sand entered the picture when Willard had to walk to the corner to procure a cab.

I quickly looked at Hughena; her grey uniform reminded me vividly of the nurses I encountered early in life when I practiced at St. John of the Cross Infirmary. My medical career suffered once Holmes and I met.

I asked my old friend, "After you handed the cash to the police what else may you have gained from that experience."

Holmes answered, "Two things, I did see a change in the city but a change in young people as well, more often they bought their homes rather than rented them.

I looked over at Hughena. She was the only one here who didn't have grey hair. A few more years of looking after Holmes and that would change, I thought with a smile. For now,

I wanted more information to keep the small gathering enlightened and entertained. I left it to Holmes to do both, like he always could and regularly did.

I did ask however, "About the valise full of money what was that like?"

"The money was wrapped loosely and carelessly, suggesting that the money was soon to be dug up by Tyler. He needed only to make the final preparations for his escape. At that time, the "where" of the escape plan was less of a mystery but with an element of uncertainty."

"But first the money to the police."

Mrs. Hudson asked, "All well and good, dear man, but how did you find out he was planning on leaving the country, or had he already been arrested. Also, word reached me that you knew if the country of destination was not Argentina then it would be Martinique in the Caribbean. Is that so, pray tell? You claimed those two countries exclusively."

"It is so," replied Holmes, "but you see both countries have no extradition treaty with Great Britain. I should also mention, the extradition treaty, means any criminal wanted by the British legal authorities could by Argentina and Martinique law, stay in those countries and be free from any interference from British officialdom. I managed to get the information by calling the passport office. It was that simple. The country of choice before all this was Argentina. The Argentinians would remain uninterested in any crime not committed on their shores.

I could see my friend carefully considering the last lingering piece of his birthday cake. Following the cake he pulled out a tin of Dunhill shag tobacco.

Holmes soon had the bowl of his pipe afire and he puffed contently. As for Holmes, an almost beatific look had come over him. He, for a brief minute or two, looked more like a forty-year-old, rather than someone just retiring. I couldn't explain it. Here was Holmes going decidedly in a completely different direction from what should be so.

Now however, it was time for the award from Scotland Yard.

The ceremony went well and all were pleased, but shortly thereafter the crowd started to entreat Holmes to get on with the story. He did go forth until near the end.

He said, "In all the excitement of the story, dear man, I forgot to present you with your Certificate of Merit. My word, you are a most fascinating man. For as long as there is a Scotland Yard you shall be remembered. Hartigan shook our hands and left."

In closing Holmes came out and said, "All that was left was to arrest this Tyler fellow. His picture had been given out frequently. It was no secret that he was a regular at the Chinaman's café, soon he was flushed out. He was no further trouble and was given severe sentence. However the terms of his parole went easier on him."

After all of that was concluded and to well wishers thinned out I had a few words with my friend, "It was a danger fraught life Holmes. We are lucky to still be here."

"In deed" he replied, but if ever a chance I would do it all over again."

I asked, "Except for?"

"Yes, next time I would be a better violinist."

Death and No Consequences

Having known my friend Sherlock Holmes for some years, I could tell by the sounds coming from upstairs that he was shaving. He was more alert than ever these past eight months. Until recently, he would still be abed at this hour. As for his pipe, he had increased his tobacco consumption this last fall till now, the Christmas season.

I could barely believe what happened next. Someone was at the door, yet it was only 7:30 AM. I went to tell the person to call at a more suitable hour. The person was Sarah MacGuillicudy. She was a personal secretary to Lord Hotchkiss, he being the nobleman who was the charge d'affaires of the Peerage Society Association. He was the watchdog to ensure protocol should a royal person misbehave or a person other than royalty, besmirch a titled member of British society. He contributed in other ways as well to make the lives of British Royalty more amenable and trouble free.

What use, pray tell, could she or Lord Hotchkiss, have for my friend of longstanding, Sherlock Holmes. On looking at young Miss MacGuillicuddy, I saw a healthy young woman.

She was well washed and dressed, with a spectacular head of blonde hair.

Holmes walked into our room, thankfully covered decently, except for his argyle, fleece-lined slippers. I performed the introductions. All hope of a quiet breakfast was soon postponed.

Holmes asked, "What moved you, Miss MacGuillicudy, to come to me?"

The woman looked over at me and asked, "Is it safe to talk, knowing that what I now tell you, must never be repeated?"

Holmes remarked, "Of course, and I'm sure I speak for the doctor as well."

"Indeed," I murmured.

Our lovely female guest gave me a piercing stare and asked, "Is that so, Doctor Watson? The reason I must be sure is, it is something that has blemished our Queen's royal court and a relative of hers is deeply involved."

Holmes, smiling, said, "Please tell us more."

With much hesitation, our early morning visitor told us how the oft-troubled Prince Henry had allegedly murdered a waitress late last night. He was a nephew of Queen Victoria and right now the investigation was not being reported. We were told only what we needed to know. Eliza insisted that Prince Henry was innocent of the charge.

Miss MacGuillicudy told us her given name was Eliza, and then informed us that the prince was a favourite of our Queen, and would not do anything half that atrocious, besides there was three other men there with him. Two were common criminals and the third his own companion, count Luis D'Arito of The Spain Royal Family.

Holmes, whose fame had spread over most of Britain, was being asked to investigate the murder, find out the reason or reasons for the murder, and whatever made Prince Henry get involved with a waitress whose immediate family were Irish immigrants and what was their relationship. However, the girl, Nellie Malone, was born in England and her father was a trained elementary school teacher and her mother, a nurse before they immigrated. My own feelings were that something was amiss here. I had no idea what. It did not change anything when Miss Eliza informed us both that this Malone female was very attractive.

This was an easy case and one that would pay well. Not

that Holmes was practical about money matters. Miss Eliza informed us that we would be paid our usual stipend by the British Peerage Society and Lord Hotchkiss would personally handle it. The more discreet we were the more generous would be our remuneration.

After Miss Eliza MacGuillicudy departed, Holmes remarked, "I am quite ravenous, Watson."

I replied, "No time for a fit breakfast. Speed is of the essence."

"What a time for my housekeeper to become sick."

I replied, "I looked in on her. It's not pneumonia but a bad case of the flu."

"So be it, Watson."

We soon were in a hansom and on our way. We were informed by young Eliza of the location of the victim, in one of the few decent Irish neighbourhood in London, where she was employed in her uncle's restaurant temporarily. It was that restaurant where her remains had been found.

Holmes still looked rather fit. Any attempt at sartorial success had been completely lost on him. His dark hair had thinned but a mere trifle but still no sign of silvery threads. His necktie couldn't be more pitiful. His thin facial features, however, drew most peoples' attention. Not that I had much to boast about. Less, since I received my second letter from the London Medical Society concerning my careless manner of managing my medical practice.

I asked my friend of many years, "Is there any way Prince Henry can be censured for his behaviour"

Holmes replied, "Indeed but for now let us hope to keep clear of the press. The case to prove his innocence will not be as shackled that way. As for his fellow royals they will hopefully stay behind him. That way the politics behind all this will not be as complex.

Our job is to find the criminals involved and therefore prove the prince's innocence. As for the police they only deal in facts and we must provide them with the right facts. The prince is very arrogant young man and hopefully this situation might make him more thoughtful. There will be a public out cry. People have a strong sense of propriety and expect the Royal family to conduct themselves in a manner fitting their standing in society."

Holmes gazed on me benignly and then put his head back as if in a trance. Still no thoughtful pipe firing but I did note there were packaged cigarettes in his shirt pocket.

Then he said, "I hope the Prince will not go to jail."

From what I could surmise this Miss Malone was an attractive young woman, with beautiful blue eyes. She worked as a legal office clerk for a barrister, who, once retired, chose to close his office rather than sell it. She was filling time until some more suitable means of employment surfaced.

Despite Holmes' concern, the case was made that much simpler; today being Sunday and the newspapers didn't publish on Sunday. Instead, other than a skeleton crew, even their printing presses were for the most part shut down. To add to the festivities, it was December 16 and stories of the season easily filled blank columns as did the necessity for more advertising space. If this was our Christmas blessing, bah, humbug.

I buttoned up the top of my overcoat, as the raw, damp, cold settled in. We had travelled through a slum area but now were in a better district. The houses were an improvement and the passers-by were better dressed and more prosperous looking. That and fewer stray dogs and cats and hardly any litter strewn about.

Once inside the restaurant, I was impressed with the accoutrements, I could tell there was no heat on. It was cool but no dampness. There was a tall, slim, blond London bobby on the premises keeping a close watch. We introduced ourselves and when we asked, he said, "No disturbances and even less bother, sirs."

I asked, "Any reporters?"

The bobby replied, "None, sir."

Holmes asked, "The remains then?"

The bobby, Randolph Grover, replied, "It's down in the basement, and well, very grotesque."

I asked, "In what way?"

"The remains were found to be dismembered, sir."

"So I have been informed. Awful," was my reply.

Holmes asked, "Can you lead us down?"

"If you would, sir, certainly."

Grover lit an oil lantern and led the way. I followed behind Holmes making note of his barely pressed, brown trousers. My years as a doctor, I felt certain, had prepared me for what was to come next.

We went into the stores room. Holmes uttered, "Oh, my God."

I took a look and started to gag. Even in a hospital setting I had never seen anything as macabre or horrifying.

Something caught my eye a short moment later. I asked, "What is that, Constable Grover or would you…well, of all…"

Grover replied, "I can answer you, sir, but because you are a man of medicine, you've likely digested it by now."

"Damn it!"

"What is it, Watson?" asked Holmes.

"I believe it's time to brush up on my medical techniques." I had just been looking at was a fetus.

"Can you estimate the age of the fetus Watson?"

In reply to Holmes' question I said, "The embryo is passed its third month and most likely close to the fourteenth week in the womb."

"Then, as you can see, we have a beast on our hands. His own jaw was set, a comment or two, on the bizarre actions and nothing more. "The law is powerless."

I replied, "Not really, barbarianism Holmes. I wonder if the Prince was aware of the pregnancy?"

Grover looked uncomfortable.

Holmes declared, "No murder weapon and other implements of brutality left behind. Clearly it was an act done by criminals of the most hard-core kind.

I replied, "There may be some redemption in sight. For now there is only evil here. Nellie will be mourned but nothing more."

Young Grover asked of Holmes, "Is there at least an attempt at justice being done?"

"There is and this case is so volatile justice may arrive soon."

Holmes replied, "This brutal act was inspired by the devil and I'm not one to lock horns with the supernatural. If I have to however I will. Holmes' eyes were glittering with anger.

We then walked back up to the restaurant accompanied on our way by the sound of small scratchy feet on their way in to sample whatever they may.

Back in the restaurant, called Morrissey's of Dingle Road, Holmes and I needed a chair. We sat at one of the tables and I soon adjusted my position to Holmes' long legs.

Grover said, "I am just going to nose about the kitchen for a bit. I'm not expecting trouble and still no reporters that I was told to stay clear of providing any commentary. A most favourable omen."

Holmes said, "We shall await your nose."

Grover replied, "Yes, sir. I should inform you, that this afternoon, three men will be arriving to remove the remains of Miss Malone. That corpse I predict will never be seen again."

Holmes remarked, the good news is Grover has gone into the kitchen.

I replied, "As well, I have been dreaming of a bowl of oatmeal all morning."

"First, here comes tea and sweet rolls."

Not long after, I did get my oatmeal and Holmes was served eggs sunny side up with fried potatoes and an unbelievable four fat German sausages. We both felt much better.

Nellie's parents, seemingly Catholic, would be thinking, likely as not, to hold a memorial service for her. Her life ended tragically and no one may ever know why.

Time, however, was heavy on our hands. I walked up near the front window. The window itself was unusual because it was divided into twenty, twelve-inch long panes of glass and just as wide. Each twelve-inch long sheet of glass, had its own frame, made from what could be either walnut or mahogany brought up from the Caribbean. It was a nice effect as were the green and black place mats. As for Holmes, he seemed to be satisfied just to sit there.

Then a booming voice bellowed, "Hear that Watson?"

"Other than your voice, nothing, Holmes.

"Listen closely."

It took a few minutes and then I did hear something. I asked, "What do you make it to be?"

Holmes replied, "We are being approached by a carriage and the prince in question may be a passenger."

"How is that so evident? I see no serious relation."

Holmes declared, "There are four horses, all of them trotting in unison and hauling a luxurious coach behind them."

"I could see trotting to perfection, but the coach, how do you surmise it to be luxurious?" I questioned Holmes.

Holmes remarked, "The horses are bearing a heavy load, not like a two -wheeled hansom. This coach has four wheels and is of the sturdiest construction."

I replied, "Therefore heavier and more expensive, which means high society may be approaching and noisily so, as you claim."

"Well, done, Watson. Soon I may be able to write the rest of my report."

"Yes, we must have tea and a chat with the Prince."

The carriage arrived, a most handsome rig. It was made of varnished wood with many layers well appliqued. The four mares were all black in colour and were big and strong with excellent, well-trained behaviour.

Then a head leaned forward and looked out the window. It was not just any head. I steeled myself for this moment. Holmes, however, wasn't at all flustered. Looking out the carriage window at us was the prince and a young man in a brown suit.

The man stepped out into the street and walked towards the first door. He quickly entered the establishment and said, "The prince's consience has been troubling him and he is upset by the death of the young woman. I am a member of his household staff and the prince told me to tell you that the other two men, other than count D'Arito, are both criminals. The prince and the Count met them when they were buying drugs. They went to the restaurant to buy some hashish. The Prince was told to be quiet about the murder or they would tell the press of their addiction to drugs.

Both royals decided to go public through you. We can only hope it does not become common knowledge.

The prince looked out and showed a handsome face with excellent teeth and well-formed lips. He was dressed in a gaudy black silk clock with a bright red lining to fend off the chilly air. His handsome features were topped off with a crown of charcoal colored hair.

Once the Prince's assistant was re-seated, he and the prince talked briefly. Then as the carriage started to roll by the prince waved at us.

Holmes remarked to me, "He had no real guidance in his life and became a shallow young man. He lacked empathy and feelings and was not worried about being criticized by the press. As far as he was concerned he could do no wrong. He did point an accusing finger at the two culprits and informed us we could not expect any more than that of him.

But the deed was done. Holmes took his seat and I across from him in-between his long slim legs. I was up against the table; my waistline was snug against my green tweed jacket, it having spread a couple of inches. I made note not to fill my plate as much.

I said, "What are we to do now Holmes?"

"Follow our orders and solve this case. Prince Henry has claimed he is innocent.

I would have liked to question him about the names of the two ne'er do wells. However such did not happen.

He did care enough however to brighten the dark shadow surrounding this case.

The first attraction must have been nellies buxom good

looks. It may have ended at that.

Mercifully came our tea.

Then Holmes lit up his first pipeful of the day.

Holmes closed his eyes and for but a brief second, I thought I saw a tear. He then began to haul on his pipe furiously until the bowl was as red as the setting sun.

I looked out at the sky and saw the clouds, one on top of the other spread thinly and in long parallel lines. On asking my learned friend, he told me it was a sign of a mild winter and early spring.

Holmes' face was more relaxed and he was about to say something when our fine friend, young Grover, came by and said, "It isn't much but supper shan't be long."

Grover came by and said, "I am slowly putting together a supper in case we are all still here."

I asked, "To what do we owe all this?"

Grover replied, "I have long yearned to spend some quality time with the most famous Sherlock Holmes. I understand you enjoy a good meal."

Holmes declared, "Good man."

Then the three of us were caught by surprise. A man had come to the door carrying a parcel. Holmes walked over and he asked, "For what reason are you here?"

He said, "I know of the corpse sir. In this bag is a camera. I used it last night undetected. The reason is the four men were under the influence of drugs. They did not even know I was there. I am the night clerk. I had just put the closed sign on the door but did not lock it because Nellie was soon leaving in a couple of minutes."

When the men came in I recognized the prince. He had been here a few times before to see Nellie. There was a friend with him and two criminals. One of the criminals I recognized was Danny Mulvany. He comes through this area trying to get girls to go to work for him as prostitutes. He became furious when Nellie turned him down.

From my hiding, the broom closet I could open it a crack and get a look and a photograph of their table.

The first photograph shows the four of them together. The second photograph shows only the prince and his friend sitting at the table. The third photo, and they are all four, together again. The fourth photograph shows that both Royals are gone and the other two are still there."

The cook Francis Murphy continued, "I can testify if need be."

I could not help but smile, the photographs were priceless.

The Prince was just given a reprieve. His good name was restored. There was Nellie of course but getting young women pregnant was not illegal. Murdering them was however. There he had only the slight taint that goes with an association with men like Mulvany. The press would flog that angle.

The photograph would have to be released and the groups use of hashish would soon be public knowledge. But it was Mulvany and his associate who would be brought up on murder charges. The condition the corpse would probably make the news in other European Centres. The kitchen helper would be grilled on that facet of the crime. It was obviously a two-man murder.

This way the prince would not be charged with being an accessory to the fact.

The crime scene had been carefully searched by the constabulary but consistent with Holmes investigative style, he was compelled to search on his own. The search included the outbuildings that acted as storerooms for the restaurant.

He stooped to pick something up from the meat locker. He took it in and we both examined it. It was an axe and there were some blood stains on it. Holmes pressed on asking me, "Is this animal or human remains?"

I replied, "Given my experience and the residual human skin on the blade, I think we have found the murder weapon."

This was another nail out of Prince Henry's coffin and would be invaluable to the defence.

Holmes said, "There it is again, the volatility caused by this situation. I can hardly explain it."

Through Grover we reported the results of our investigation to the police. Holmes and I rested easily knowing we had the evidence needed to implicate the killers.

Grover said, "The police lieutenant has asked you to wait. It should be for no longer than a half an hour." We both agreed we would wait and not long after two middle aged men walked in. The taller of the two had a slight limp. He said, "You have done well."

The next hour or so was spent sharing information and

an examination of the incriminating photographs.

On the way back to our homes I asked, "It is my imagination or will the prince avoid going to jail."

Holmes replied, "Ordinarily yes but I have just thought of a new charge he could well be prosecuted for."

I asked, "But what would it possibly be?"

Holmes replied, "A charge of withholding evidence."

"I see your point." I said.

Holmes declared, "That charge could lead to a few months in jail but unlikely for a member of the Royal family. As happens way too often during the course of our history, death with no consequences."

I declared, "But look at us. We are now on Baker Street. There is our place up ahead. Despite a world in turmoil, once more we have arrived home and still in good condition."

The Man Who Was Too Greedy

Holmes' phone rang and since he wasn't quite finished his morning tea, I answered.

A young female voice asked, "Mr. Holmes?"

"Not quite, I am Dr. Watson, a friend and confrere."

The articulate voice stated, "I must speak to Detective Holmes immediately, if it is at all possible."

"I shall speak to Mr. Holmes on your behalf."

My old friend Sherlock Holmes paused to light a cigarette and then picked up the receiver. He said, "Yes, what is it now?"

The woman answered, "Firstly my name is Julia Anderson. I am the confidential secretary of Lady Ophelia Breckinridge, wife of Lord Harrington Breckinridge, he being a member of the House of Lords. May I come by to see you Mr. Holmes?"

"By all means Miss Anderson."

A time was set for one hour from the phone call.

Soon enough she arrived and had been seated.

Holmes asked, "Since you want to see me what are the particulars that you feel I can help you with please go on."

Holmes had judged her as a woman who would prefer to get to the business at hand.

Miss Julia said, "Allowing for who I am employed by, I must tell you that this is to go no further."

Certainly, Doctor Watson and I will be happy to respect your wishes.

"Ah, well, I see, please continue on, if you would be so kind."

Miss Julia in an emotional voice of some consternation replied, "I shall come right out with these very unpleasant facts in hope on my part, and the Breckinridge family, that you can set this ugly matter to right. You and your partner came highly recommended to the family. The problem is some valuable black pearls were recently stolen. Not here in England but in Papeete Tahiti. We approached Scotland Yard for help but the location of the crime dictated a negative response. You were recommended and we were informed that you are quite discreet. The pearls are the property of Mrs. Marta Starman, wife of

Oracle Starman, who owns extensive diamond and gold holdings in South Africa. The pearls were to be held by Lady Breckinridge until Mrs. Starman came to London in advance of the wedding.

What has bonded the two women is that Lady Breckinridge's daughter Nancy is to be married to Stuart Starman, the son of Marta and Oracle Starman. Both sets of parents are heartily in favour of the match, soon to be consummated in marriage. It is considered to be the society event of the season. Even one of Queen Victoria's grandchildren is going to be present. The family wants nothing to mar the celebration.

The missing pearls were to be sewn on to the dress that Mrs. Starman was going to wear to the wedding ceremony.

Mr. Opi Glun telegraphed us in early August informing us of the theft. A second cable followed the next day. I shall get to the reason for the second cable in a few minutes. However, since then we heard nothing so we tried contacting Mr. Glun over the next two days but we were unable to reach him.

Holmes said, "This is all quite interesting. From here it seems like a warm, caressing, blue velvet day. Blue Velvet is the incredible Blue Sky, but please continue on."

"Thank you, we know who committed the theft, the result of a few moments of carelessness on Mr. Glun's part. It was a Tahitian prostitute, a quick impulsive spur of the moment robbery, when Opi Glun, the broker, turned his back on the pouch full of black pearls. He had placed them on his desk near the open window of his office on Waterfront Road."

The urgency of her words without a slightest pause of variance made Holmes and I aware that this was a very important matter beyond the level of stolen property.

Holmes asked, "Where does this information come from?"

Miss Julia replied, "The reason why there was a second telegram full of more facts was because that same night of the robbery the remains of the prostitute had been found. She was bludgeoned to death."

We know she dated merchant seamen and had a sailor boyfriend called Mike, an American sailor who was in port at the time. Mr. Glun informed us he is going to turn the matter over to the French Surete who handle criminal matters for French Polynesia. Since then we've had no contact with him. I did not know why but here I am, Mr. Holmes, hoping you may be able to be of some help.

There was an American registered ship in port at the time. There are many ships that use the Papeete Harbour but this one ship was on its way to Hong Kong where they were to receive a shipment of silk and unload a shipment of guano, a bird droppings fertilizer gathered in the South Pacific and sold in Hong Kong where the rice farmers find it a potent fertilizer. There are other markets for it as well; all this information came from Mr. Glun.

The way the pearls suddenly disappeared from the island alarmed Opi Glun even more so. He asked around as best he could after reporting the theft to the French Surete, and found out the Oleander, the American owned ship, had shipped out a couple of hours after the theft with the American Sailor, Mike the boyfriend on board. Besides silk in Hong Kong, they were also to sail to New Zealand to pick up a shipment of wool in Wellington. The next stop after New Zealand was Plymouth Harbour here in England where the wool and silk was to be unloaded.

That was the last time we heard from Mr. Glun despite trying to contact him. Not quite knowing what to do we contacted you.

Holmes pondered the information and offered some early thinking. The pearls should be safe until they arrive in England. The culprit's cunning, his intelligence, should make it clear to him that a fence, as they call these men who buy stolen goods, would pay more in the U.K. than he could hope to get for the pearls in Hong Kong. No doubt the thief would prefer to be paid in hard currency rather than Hong Kong dollars.

Miss. Julia Anderson asked, "So can you be of some assistance to the Breckinridge family, Mr. Holmes?"

Holmes had a faraway look in his eyes. Then he said, "I am sure Tahiti has its own police, whose help I may need, but being unable to contact Mr. Glun is meaningless in itself. The criminals are coming our way."

I could not help but interject, "Surely some contact will be needed Holmes."

Holmes' eyes bored directly into mine. He said, "It is hurricane season in that part of the world. That part of the world has problems with monsoons and typhoons and many other such hardships during this time of year. The winds will often have a velocity of seventy-five miles per hour. It stands to reason that the telegraph system received some damage. I shall try to contact the French navy through my friends in the embassy. I am owed a few favours in that world but that is a story for another time. It stands to reason that they would have their own private telegraph system. A communication facility is one more way that the nation is prepared for a war. Before I try the French military I shall try the French Surete in case there has been new developments in this case. If nothing else they could explain why we have lost communication with the island.

Miss Julia Anderson replied, "I'm so happy that you will intercede for the Breckinridge family. Lady Breckinridge had promised to look after the pearls until Mrs. Starman arrived here for her dress fittings. She prefers to use a Canadian dress designer now in London. Also, the time spent at the Breckinridge Estate should prove to be a chance for both women to get to know each other. They are soon to be related after all."

"I shall intercede of course. It will be a challenge, but I shall try and unravel this criminal act, and expose the culprit."

Holmes then switched tactics. He asked, "As of this affair of the heart does it speak of permanence?"

"Very much so," Miss Julia replied. "There has been no

change in their ardour."

"Delightful," I interjected. I wanted to take part in the excitement.

Miss Julia continued, "Stuart has other worries. The other problem besetting him so is his father Oracle Starman wants Stuart to work in the family's gold holdings in the Witwatersrand Gold Field as discovered by George Harrison some years ago. The holdings are quite vast actually, although the Starman owned mine is a more junior player, such a massive discovery made Mr. Starman wealthy.

Then there is Mr. Starman's interest in the De Beers diamond fields. Mr. Starman realized enough money from his stake in his diamond venture to invest some of the profits in the Witwatersrand Gold Field."

Holmes declared, "We are speaking of some wealth here."

"Yes and Oracle Starman wants him to work in the gold fields."

Holmes replied, "Well this Stuart sounds headstrong enough."

Miss Julia replied, "He is young yet, but he is close to his family and a gold mine is a worth a good sized fortune."

Miss Julia continued. "Johannesburg in the north is connected to Cape Town in the south by a well-constructed highway. Cape Town is a city of some opulence and is near Kimberly where the diamond discovery took place. Kimberly is where Stuart would like to work. He may end up working in the office in Cape Town, but that remains to be seen.

The beaches are supposed to be beautiful there in the warm south Atlantic water. That would make an excellent vacation spot for the young couple."

Holmes, tired of all this romanticizing, said, "Well, either family could easily absorb the financial loss covering the pearls so why such consternation unless the pearls are vitally necessary for some other reason."

Miss Julia's face registered a look of amusement.

She stated, "As you may have guessed there will be a lot of bejewelled women throughout the whole affair, especially diamonds. Actually, it seems Mrs. Starman has an allergy to diamonds. She is afraid she may break out or become effluvial. The black pearls were to be sewn onto the neckline of her dress as a replacement for a diamond necklace that most of the other guests will quite likely wear. The remaining pearls were to make a matching pattern on her upper sleeves. The rest of her jewellery will be of an assortment of other precious gems but not a single diamond."

As an M.D. despite not practicing much, as Holmes and I had become busier, I had to say, "During my medical studies I never heard of such an allergy. I do not quite see how it could be possible."

Miss Julia replied, "Well, God forbid I get caught saying this, but her family, mainly Stuart, describes her allergy as being caused by eating too many Boerewors. They are sausages made by some farmers not far outside of Cape Town. Mrs. Starman always denied that she was allergic to Boerewors, she likes them that much. It is a minor allergy mind you but she keeps insisting the allergic reaction is caused by contact with diamonds."

It was her husband Oracle who took her to Cape Town. There is a part of the city set aside for the more luxurious homes and the sort of people who can afford to live quite well. The ocean breezes are refreshing but the sun is hot enough to bake the rich land but benignly so.

Holmes said, "So the pearls would substitute or perhaps make amends for the more customary diamonds whether her son and husband like it or not."

In a simple manner, Holmes described the heart of the matter but with more to follow no doubt.

Holmes continued, "An idiosyncrasy on Mrs. Starman's part but it does not stop making the pearls invaluable to her however."

"Quite so," Miss Julia remarked. Then she continued, "We have turned to you because we have not heard from Opi Glun in four days since the evening of August 8th."

Holmes looked at his calendar thoughtfully. Then he sat more upright in his chair. He said, "By Jove, thanks to the BBC, I remember that there was a nasty hurricane in French Polynesia around that time. I believe it was August 8th because that same broadcast carried news of labour unrest in Leeds. Then of course there are time zones to consider. Quickly calculating when you received the telegram on August 8th it would be August 9th in Tahiti. Of course, to send a telegraph this far Opi Glun must have just missed the hurricane by a couple of hours. The mathematics works."

With winds of 75 miles an hour the telegraphy system must have been too damaged to stay in operation. In the meantime, I will try the French Surete and also the French naval base in that area. They both could have wireless systems that operate independently of the one used by the general telegrapher's office."

Miss Julia remarked, "Of all times for a hurricane to strike. Tell me, Dr. Watson, as an educated man, do you know what causes such fierce storms?"

I replied, "It all depends on the barometric pressure. If it is low enough expect a hurricane. Is that not so, Holmes?"

"Quite so Watson, but now they are finding that water temperature may also play a part in these severe storms."

Miss Julia remarked, "Four days ago is a long time, surely this Glun fellow would have the ability to communicate with us by now?"

Holmes replied, "Despite that I shall try to raise the French Surete. They may have their own telegraphy equipment. They could prove to be of some aid to a plan I am starting to sketch in my mind. Do not get me wrong, immediately after our chat ends I shall go to work on this very important case, and one of the first people I am hoping to contact is Opi Glun."

Miss Julia said, "My mind is starting to be cleared of cobwebs. I hope you can keep doing so. It has been stressful. The reason why I am here is that Lady Breckinridge insisted I go to you. She is familiar with you because of the time you proved that the son of a friend of hers was absolutely not guilty of drug smuggling by using his yacht. She told me your mind is most formidable."

"Thank you, Miss Anderson, by now there must be something up and running, so I shall draft a telegram with a lot of questions and I shall want answers. Then if all goes well I shall soon have a trap ready but one needing some bait. I can set it and hopefully snare the game; in this case, a good-sized rat."

Miss Julia said, "So here I am suddenly quite useless to the both of you."

I replied, "Not in the least and I am sure my friend here seconds my opinion you have brightened our day."

"Well thank you, Dr. Watson, if there is anything I can do."

Holmes replied, "There is Julia, if I may call you that. Perhaps you could leave your contact information with me. I may have some need of your assistance and soon. Also does her ladyship carry insurance?"

"Yes, with Holsted."

"I see," Holmes replied tersely.

Shortly after Miss Anderson left the premises.

Holmes spent close to half an hour carefully drafting a cable to the police department in Papeete. He phoned in the cablegram to the London Telegraphy Office. They courteously called him back to tell him the telegraph system was once more in running order.

At just past noon the next day, a delivery boy from the telegraph office travelling by bicycle delivered a reply addressed to Detective Sherlock Holmes on Baker Street. Holmes was going to read it right away but decided first to have a pipe full. He seemed assured, perhaps too optimistic.

I went into the kitchen to finish my sweet roll and tea. I was barely finished when Holmes came roaring in.

He asked, "Are you ready Watson?"

I replied, "Yes, but for what?"

Holmes replied, "I must immediately attempt to contact

the office manager of Holsted Insurance. I should tell you first, that the prostitute turned thief was found murdered in very recent times but you are aware of that no doubt. That may complicate matters. The last man to see her alive was a sailor called Mike. No last name. He is an American on the American flagged ship 'The Oleander.' You no doubt have an inkling of the ship in question. The ship left port an hour or two after Mr. Glun reported the robbery."

Holmes continued, "I grant you that there is no insurance claim since the pearls didn't make it to here. It is an entirely different reason why I want to visit the office of Holsted Insurance."

"Oh."

Holmes went on, "I will ensure that the manager is aware that I am working for some wealthy and influential people. Certainly, Lord and Lady Breckinridge but also the Starmans, especially Mr. Oracle Starman. Let us get to it immediately and hope that some of the reflected aura rubs off on us and impresses the insurance people.

I replied to my distinguished friend, "I have never considered myself motley. However, since you are up to something I shall be happy to accompany you. I am reasonably sure that the people at Holsted will give you a listen, after which we should be able to leave their premises on our own rather than get run off the property."

I dabbed a serviette around my mouth and did a quick inspection of my hands. I then said, "I am at your disposal."

After a bit we arrived at the Holsted building where we were shown to a waiting room. Shortly a senior claims adjustor interviewed us.

Holmes carefully explained himself and our need of help from the Holsted Insurance firm. He made good mention of the family we were retained by.

After that another senior claims adjustor came by to appraise us. Holmes wasn't sure but he felt strongly that Holsted hadn't insured the pearls. Holmes explained what he needed to recover the pearls and have the thief put in jail. This senior adjustor had gone to the general manager told the adjustor that he would stand by his actions. That made it much easier for Mr. Dillon the new claims adjustor to decide. Holsted was chosen by Holmes to play a part in the rattrap by baiting the trap with a large sum of money. That much money in British pounds would lure our thief to a trap that was so richly set. What the thief would not know was the money was counterfeit. Holmes explained his plan clearly to Mr. Dillon, and suggested that, based on years of experience, the plan will work.

The insurance man chosen for setting the trap needed to be ready to travel to Plymouth on short notice and must be well attired. He would need a satchel to hold the money. The thief needed only to hand over the pearls and in receipt he would get the fake payment. Not that it mattered because after that phony deal was transacted he would be arrested. Whether the pearls were insured or not didn't matter.

The plan saw Holmes place an ad in the personal column of the Wellington, New Zealand newspaper. Wellington was the heart of sheep sales in New Zealand, including wool. There was a shipyard there as well. Holmes explained all this to Mr. Dillon and then said, "New Zealand is covered in sheep flocks and Wellington is the capital city of New Zealand, a member in good standing of the British Empire. If the ship needs a few repairs the shipyard in Wellington should be able to handle it. And of course the wool."

Mr. Dillon replied, "Why are you so sure this Mike will bite. He may not even read the papers." Mr. Dillon seemed in a doubtful mood. Could Holmes change all that? There was always the general manager.

Detective Holmes said, "There is a camaraderie among sailors. More than one of them who read that paper would tell the alleged thief Mike about the ad. Mike is a sailor, so his friends amongst the shipmates could tell he was involved in a criminal act. They would only wish him well. He may even have a confidante on board that he told secrets to."

Holmes explained, "The lucrative offer outlined in the New Zealand AU will have Plymouth contact information. It is imperative that our thief Mike does not try to sell the pearls prior to arriving in Plymouth."

Mr. Dillon somewhat placated said, "I am not yet convinced but it may work.

Mr. Dillon still not accepting the idea fully did say, "Well, it's all we have to go on so you, Mr. Holmes, can place the ad and bait the trap. I will have one of my sales agents placed at your disposal for the pay off. Make sure in the ad that you stipulate private deal only so that a certain well-to-do woman who wants to avoid all scandal recovers the precious, black pearls.

Holmes replied, "Yes, you do understand the plan. We will use the ad to lure our thief to Plymouth where we will be waiting."

Holmes thought briefly and said, "The allure of easy money is one thing but I suspect that our man Mike may see a chance to pull a double cross. If so I shall counter with a triple cross. I have not forgotten that prostitute he murdered out of greed. To him it was an effortless and uncomplicated way to handle the theft with all the profits going to him. He is not capable of relating to people in a normal decent way. He has no imagination. I say we will fool him."

Then Holmes asked, "Are the pearls at all insured?"

Dillon replied, "That is confidential information between her ladyship and Holsted.

Mr. Dillon returned to his work and Holmes and I were soon shown the way out. We had an agreement in principle with Mr. Dillon and Holsted Insurance.

I said to Holmes, "Shortly after we get back to Baker Street remind me to call the shipping office. They may have some way of notifying us on the movements of the Oleander."

"Stellar idea Watson; as for this sailor Mike, greed will

be his undoing. I am assuming that our Mike felon is not a sophisticated criminal."

I answered by saying, "Yes, he may be susceptible to the easy money of your plan."

The next stop after Holsted was to Scotland Yard where a certain Inspector Bradley was expecting us.

In the telegram my friend Holmes had received earlier from the French Polynesian Surete there was some new information. Of course, Holmes's concurrent theories being affirmed as correct.

The prostitute had been battered severely and then stabbed to death and this Mike dated her regularly when he was in port. His ship was in port that day but left two hours or so after the murder. His ship the 'Oleander' was an American flagged ship and New York its homeport.

Once the two of us, after travelling by hansom, were sitting comfortably in Inspector Bradley's office, our plan was explained in detail. Holmes and Bradley got along well and spent the first 30 minutes discussing Holmes' cases that Bradley had followed closely. It was all very congenial.

Bradley seemed to concur with Holmes well baited trap.

Bradley mentioned, "An arrest in New Zealand may jeopardize the recovery of the pearls. Between the Breckinridge family and the Starman's I am at your disposal. I don't say that every day."

Bradley continued, "As for Mrs. Breckinridge I plan to give you full reign over the case you cross borders easier than I. Beside which the family has you on retainer after all and we can support you in the background very discreetly until called upon. Holmes, it appears to me you have a decent chance to rescue the pearls. I should add the trip from here to Plymouth by train is twelve hours long."

Let us not forget where her husband, Lord Breckinridge, toils and for the good of Britain and all subjects to the crown."

Holmes tentatively inquired, "Then you are willing to meet me in Plymouth, hopefully just before the Oleander docks. If the wait is longer, I shan't complain."

Bradley replied, "Keep me posted if you can on the ship's movements and I shall ask our Plymouth office to watch for the ship as well."

Holmes said, "If all goes well we should all meet in the customs' shed for disembarking passengers. Sailors are likely rushed through. If I can ask one last favour of you Inspector?"

"Certainly."

"Remember your comment about staying in the background if you can, until I expose this Mike for what it is worth. Also bring in a couple of strong, physically fit plainclothes men.

This Mike may try running and fisticuffs I hardly rule out. He is a strong man and allowing for what prisons are like, I do not rule out an attempt to escape."

After we left, I asked Holmes, "Time for tea?"

Holmes answered, "We are only getting started, Doctor, first a trip to the shipping office."

At the shipping office, we went through the usual channels that the British civil servants expect people to do. We were told that Watson's and Holmes' request for service would be granted. Perhaps I had noticed just a hint of recognition on the young clerk's face when my friend, the well-known sleuth, mentioned his name. The civil servant did give us information on the number of days of sailing time it would take to leave New Zealand and sail through to Plymouth, England. It was a long sail and depended on the seas and headwinds. There wasn't much to do now but wait. For now, all that was necessary was to place an advertisement in the Wellington daily paper concerning the purchase of the pilfered and blood stained pearls. The murderer and thief may be on his way there already. Holmes would try and discreetly word, in between the lines, the insurance company angle and no police involvement. The family in question wanted the pearls back. Everything else, Holmes would suggest, was unimportant. Holmes, on remembering the different time zone in New Zealand, allowed for that when placing the ad for three days.

It was now time to wait. During that time, we met Mr. Cummings who was chosen by the insurance executive, Mr. Dillon, to assist Holmes and I in the case. We put him through a rehearsal and then told him to be available when the Oleander arrives. All was set but would it work?

During the intervening days spent waiting for the ship, Holmes and I used the time productively. We both straightened out a few matters that needed some attention and I had a few letters to write. Until a few years ago I would have reopened my medical office and treated any of my patients who may have been happy to see me back in my M.D's harness.

However, these past four years in particular, I had

become so caught up in my friend's, the great detective's work, that my medical practice was a mere memory. Detective work did have its rewards and it had always pained me, when no matter what I tried as a physician, the disease in question couldn't be successfully treated. Good detective work rarely saw me finish a case still frustrated.

With great relief, our anticipated response from Seaman Mike arrived by post. He was indeed taking the New Zealand offer seriously. Our thief did not admit to possessing the valued jewels. He indicated that he had information that would help us secure the pearls in a timely manner. Seaman Mike was naïve as to his expected arrival enough to volunteer the information in Plymouth Harbour. He also promised the level of confidentiality the "great family" so desired. According to Seaman Mike, two payments were necessary. First, he would need to be paid for the information. Secondly, the reward offered, would need to be paid in accordance with the New Zealand newspaper advertisement. In other words the payment for the pearls in question. He also agreed that he would put up with the family's expert on the value of the pearls. That would be Doctor Watson. The Breckingridge's would of course want proof that they were getting fair value for their money.

The thought worked.

Then word reached us from the shipping office that the Oleander was not sixteen hours sailing from Plymouth. The ad placed in the Wellington paper stipulated that the contact would take place in Plymouth. Holmes knew early on that was where the ship was going to unload its wool. It would not take before the merchant vessel with its cargo on board would be docking. The ship, however, was still some distance south of England. There was an extra two hours' leeway on our part because sea captains didn't grant shore leave until the ship had been secured in port for at least two hours. The shipping office had passed that on to Holmes for his planning.

Detective Sherlock Holmes then placed a call to the Plymouth Port Authority. The information he received was of some help; it included the jetty number that the ship would be birthed at and approximately what time the ship would tie up. There was ample time to get to Plymouth. Holmes soon had our party rounded up and we all were to meet in the same location, the visitors' section of the customs and tariffs building. The ship had made such good time I presumed the sailors, from New Zealand around the southerly end of Africa into the Atlantic waters, and up to the coast of Europe, must have had some easy sailing with no more weather-related problems. As they did in the South Seas.

We made it to Plymouth and soon sketched out a plan we thought would work.

We were down to a half an hour before the ship let the sailors go ashore. His final word on the subject was not to act until requested by him. The plainclothes officers were positioned away from the search area. One covered one side of Inspector Bradley and the other officer sat ready some distance away. Standing to Holmes right hand side was Mr. Cummings. Mr. Cummings, Edwin, his first name, was the one most visible from the customs inspection area and the satchel was clearly displayed without being too obvious.

Holmes quickly remarked, "The sailor in question I have had described to me via a second telegram, is tall, a wiry build and still a strong man. He has a ruddy complexion, long thinning light brown hair, and with small blue eyes. Be prepared. The French Surete, Polynesia District, think they have enough to charge him with murder and they are still actively working on the murder case. We may be able to help there."

Shortly, sailors started to enter the customs area

designated for sailors only. The Scotland Yard inspector, Thomas Bradley, acted like a man engrossed in the local Plymouth newspaper. We were in our own separate ways ready for action. Mike passed customs easily.

When he saw Mr. Cummings he smiled. Intuitively, Seaman Mike recognized the dress of Mr. Cummings as someone who did not belong on the docks of Plymouth. Mr. Cummings raised the satchel suggesting that the money was here and he was ready to do business.

As Holmes and Cummings moved away to create a little privacy, Mr. Cummings asked, "Do you have any goods from overseas I may want to buy?"

I followed the two of them.

Mike angrily asked, "Who is our shadow?" Mr. Cummings replied, "Yes he knows jewellery and the family asked him to check to be sure of the quality of your   ."

Mike replied, "Anymore crap and this deal is off."

Mike continued, "As you can see pretty little thing forty in number."

"Delightful," Edwin Cummings replied. "May I see a

small sampler. Money will be no problem and it is to excess.

Mike tentatively backed off a couple of short paces and said, "You cannot trust anyone but I shall give your eyes a feast."

He took out from under a faded, mid grey, summer jacket, a cloth sack with tight drawstrings keeping it closed. He loosened the drawstrings and showed ever so quickly a collection of round black objects. Holmes from ten feet away said in a low voice, "I am with the family as well." "If you would be kind enough to hold on to that bag for a couple of more minutes. I see a policewoman near the rear exit. I think she's getting ready to leave. The family asked me to double check everything.

Cummings blurted out, "I can vouch for the money. All of it in easily spendable pound notes."

I could not help wondering why Holmes did not clinch the deal and that way a murderer and thief would be locked away in prison. What was happening here?

A minute passed by, and it was a long minute. Holmes suddenly lunged at another sailor, this one very well dressed, who had just cleared customs, one place behind Mike.

He was a small man with dark, curly hair, and dark eyes.

Holmes and his team leapt into action and apprehended the youngish, dark haired sailor. Mike in the meantime, knowing it was trouble, had made a run for the back exit. Holmes shouted to both plainclothesmen, quickly now, collar him.

A search of the well-dressed, young sailor turned up the missing pearls in the bottom of a cigar box, the top layer being cigars that covered the pearls. There on top of the cigars was the address of a bordello in downtown Plymouth, and several American dollars. As sailors, the customs officers will usually give them a quick pass, for they know the sailors will soon leave the country again.

After a brief glance at the subdued Mike now looking rather sullen, I asked Holmes, "Was this the way you expected Mike's double cross to work?"

"Yes, approximately, Watson, right down to the fake pearls he presented to our Mr. Cummings. The double cross was get the money and keep the real pearls to sell again. No real imagination at work.

My double cross was to bait the rattrap for him to bite into and because of that he should be sent to prison for some years on that crime. Then there are charges facing him in Papeete but he will have to answer for this crime first."

I replied, "As you said, greed will lead to his downfall."

"Yes, that and stupidity."

Mike, whose last name came up in his American identification, was Mike Kinnerd. He was marched over to Inspector Bradley who did a quick search of him for anything else illegal. Holmes took out the cloth bag Mike had first proffered to Cummings, the insurance man, and took out a couple of the dark round objects. He threw one on the floor and after a sharp clinking sound it started to roll away. He then wetted his handkerchief with his saliva and used it to rub one of the dark round objects. The handkerchief was soon stained heavily with a black colour. Holmes then sniffed the object and then took a slight taste of it.

He said, "Black shoe polish used to coat the children's delight, a bag of marbles. He must have considered us to be of his own low mentality." But then he probably considers himself to be quite intelligent."

Inspector Bradley added, "On my part I found a knife on this Mike Kinnerd fellow. It's since been washed off but I did find a couple of reddish stains just below the hilt on the blade. If it can be determined as human blood it will be damning evidence in the potential trial concerning the murder of the Tahitian prostitute."

We all enjoyed how easily the well-baited trap, as set up by Sherlock Holmes, had caught the thief Mike, and his accomplice. Three days in the planning out over in thirty minutes of less. It was Mike though who would soon have to face murder charges followed by charges related to the theft of the pearls Here in Britain he would have to face fraud and embezzlement charges. On top of that was the charge of smuggling contraband jewellery. He would never sail again after that many years in prison all of which should leave him ruined for life. His passport finally identified him as Michael Riley and his accomplice was a fellow American, Vito Riccatoni, the son of Italian immigrants. In the meantime, Bradley had gone looking for a phone.

I asked my friend, "How could you tell that it was the other man, who seemed innocuous to me, was involved in the smuggling as well?" Because Riccatoni was well dressed. Sailors do not make much money.

Clothes are not very expensive in Hong Kong but there

was extra money for cigars with the original payoff and charge left over. The rest of the money to come in Plymouth. From there, off to the Bordello and then pocket what was left for a good time when he was back in New York. The cigar box did double duty. He saved enough cigars to hide the pearls. The promise of getting rich led him on. The Riccatoni has just become a common criminal all because he likes clothes."

"Not only that," replied Homes, "but he was also involved in the attempted swindle; because of that, not many judges would find a reason for leniency.

The smuggling and theft charges will be prosecuted here in Britain but the murder charge will have to be dealt with in Tahiti. I am sure there is a prison somewhere in the French owned Polynesian Islands that can find room for Mr. Riley. For now, it is a question of whether Britain or Tahiti has the first go at him. It all depends on who has the jurisdiction rights."

I replied, "But surely murder will outweigh theft?"

"The courts will have to straighten that matter out."

I mentioned to Holmes, "Apparently, our man Bradley will be delivering the pearls directly to the Breckinridge estate and under police protection. How fortunes change. Only yesterday they weren't welcome. The good news apparently has travelled all the way to the Breckinridge mansion."

"Oh, well, we missed a chance to see that rather impressive property would you not say Watson?"

I replied, "What would impress me just as much is a hot cup of tea and a chance to put my feet up."

"Indeed," Holmes replied, "and I should tell you that I was previously informed that if the pearls were recovered then we could expect our retainer to be generous indeed."

I replied, "Mayhap then, under those circumstances I shall have a second cup."

"Me, I am thinking of a nip of something a little stronger," Holmes declared emphatically.

Also from MX Publishing

MX Publishing is the world's largest specialist Sherlock Holmes publisher, with over a hundred titles and fifty authors creating the latest in Sherlock Holmes fiction and non-fiction.

From traditional short stories and novels to travel guides and quiz books, MX Publishing caters for all Holmes fans.

The collection includes leading titles such as *Benedict Cumberbatch In Transition* and *The Norwood Author* which won the 2011 Howlett Award (Sherlock Holmes Book of the Year).

MX Publishing also has one of the largest communities of Holmes fans on Facebook with regular contributions from dozens of authors.

www.mxpublishing.com

Also from MX Publishing

"Phil Growick's, 'The Secret Journal of Dr Watson', is an adventure which takes place in the latter part of Holmes and Watson's lives. They are entrusted by HM Government (although not officially) and the King no less to undertake a rescue mission to save the Romanovs, Russia's Royal family from a grisly end at the hand of the Bolsheviks. There is a wealth of detail in the story but not so much as would detract us from the enjoyment of the story. Espionage, counter-espionage, the ace of spies himself, double-agents, double-crossers...all these flit across the pages in a realistic and exciting way. All the characters are extremely well-drawn and Mr Growick, most importantly, does not falter with a very good ear for Holmesian dialogue indeed. Highly recommended. A five-star effort."
The Baker Street Society

www.mxpublishing.com

Also from MX Publishing

The Missing Authors Series

Sherlock Holmes and The Adventure of The Grinning Cat
Sherlock Holmes and The Nautilus Adventure
Sherlock Holmes and The Round Table Adventure

"Joseph Svec, III is brilliant in entwining two endearing and enduring classics of literature, blending the factual with the fantastical; the playful with the pensive; and the mischievous with the mysterious. We shall, all of us young and old, benefit with a cup of tea, a tranquil afternoon, and a copy of Sherlock Holmes, The Adventure of the Grinning Cat."
Amador County Holmes Hounds Sherlockian Society

www.mxpublishing.com

Also from MX Publishing

The American Literati Series

The Final Page of Baker Street
The Baron of Brede Place
Seventeen Minutes To Baker Street

"The really amazing thing about this book is the author's ability to call up the 'essence' of both the Baker Street 'digs' of Holmes and Watson as well as that of the 'mean streets' of Marlowe's Los Angeles. Although none of the action takes place in either place, Holmes and Watson share a sense of camaraderie and self-confidence in facing threats and problems that also pervades many of the later tales in the Canon. Following their conversations and banter is a return to Edwardian England and its certainties and hope for the future. This is definitely the world before The Great War."
Philip K Jones

www.mxpublishing.com

Also from MX Publishing

The Detective and The Woman Series

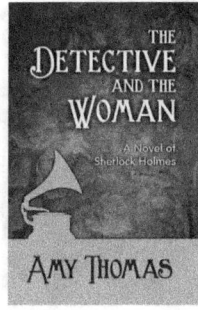  

The Detective and The Woman
The Detective, The Woman and The Winking Tree
The Detective, The Woman and The Silent Hive

"The book is entertaining, puzzling and a lot of fun. I believe the author has hit on the only type of long-term relationship possible for Sherlock Holmes and Irene Adler. The details of the narrative only add force to the romantic defects we expect in both of them and their growth and development are truly marvelous to watch. This is not a love story. Instead, it is a coming-of-age tale starring two of our favorite characters."
Philip K Jones

www.mxpublishing.com

Also from MX Publishing

Sherlock Holmes novellas in verse

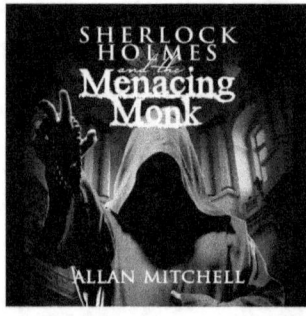

All four novellas
have been
released also in
audio format
with narration
by Steve White

Sherlock Holmes and The Menacing Moors
Sherlock Holmes and The Menacing Metropolis
Sherlock Holmes and The Menacing Melbournian
Sherlock Holmes and The Menacing Monk

"The story is really good and the Herculean effort it must have been to write it all in verse—well, my hat is off to you, Mr. Allan Mitchell! I wouldn't dream of seeing such work get less than five plus stars from me..." **The Raven**

Also from MX Publishing

When the papal apartments are burgled in 1901, Sherlock Holmes is summoned to Rome by Pope Leo XII. After learning from the pontiff that several priceless cameos that could prove compromising to the church, and perhaps determine the future of the newly unified Italy, have been stolen, Holmes is asked to recover them. In a parallel story, Michelangelo, the toast of Rome in 1501 after the unveiling of his Pieta, is commissioned by Pope Alexander VI, the last of the Borgia pontiffs, with creating the cameos that will bedevil Holmes and the papacy four centuries later. For fans of Conan Doyle's immortal detective, the game is always afoot. However, the great detective has never encountered an adversary quite like the one with whom he crosses swords in "The Vatican Cameos.."

"An extravagantly imagined and beautifully written Holmes story"
(Lee Child, NY Times Bestselling author, Jack Reacher series)